D0395074

KILL
SWITCH

ALSO BY CHRIS LYNCH

Inexcusable

Angry Young Man

KILL SWITCH

CHRIS LYNCH

SIMON & SCHUSTER BFYR

New York London Toronto Sydney New Delhi

SIMON & SCHUSTER BOOKS FOR YOUNG READERS
An imprint of Simon & Schuster Children's Publishing Division
1230 Avenue of the Americas, New York, New York 10020

This book is a work of fiction. Any references to historical events, real people, or real locales are used fictitiously. Other names, characters, places, and incidents are products of the author's imagination, and any resemblance to actual events or locales or persons, living or dead, is entirely coincidental.

Copyright © 2012 by Chris Lynch
All rights reserved, including the right of reproduction in whole or in part in any form.

SIMON & SCHUSTER BFYR is a trademark of Simon & Schuster, Inc.
For information about special discounts for bulk purchases, please contact Simon & Schuster Special Sales at 1-866-506-1949 or business@simonandschuster.com.
The Simon & Schuster Speakers Bureau can bring authors to your live event. For more information or to book an event, contact the Simon & Schuster Speakers Bureau at 1-866-248-3049 or visit our website at www.simonspeakers.com.
Book design by Krista Vossen
The text for this book is set in Berling.
Manufactured in the United States of America
2 4 6 8 10 9 7 5 3 1
Library of Congress Cataloging-in-Publication Data
Lynch, Chris, 1962–
Kill switch / Chris Lynch.
p. cm.
Summary: Daniel simply wants to spend one last summer with his grandfather, Da, before his move to college and Da's dementia pull them apart, but when Da starts to let things slip about a secret life, Daniel must protect him from old "friends" who intend to make sure Da stays quiet.
ISBN 978-1-4169-2702-0
[1. Grandfathers—Fiction. 2. Memory—Fiction. 3. Old age—Fiction.] I. Title.
PZ7.L979739Kil 2012
[Fic]—dc22
2010047773
ISBN 978-1-4424-3640-4 (eBook)

FIRST
EDITION

To Jeannie and Murph—
Here's to life, rebooted

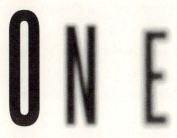

ONE

I love my Da to bits.

Which will probably come in handy, as bits is what he's in.

Da is my grandfather. He wears a MedicAlert bracelet, copper, that reads, MEMORY LOSS. He asks what it is a couple of times a day. I tell him. He's cool with it.

Because he is a cool grandfather, always was. Retired early from some government job that was something like systems analyst for the Department of Agriculture. Never, ever talked about his work. Might have been because who in his right mind would ever have bothered to ask about a job as boring as that? Might have been.

Retired early, because he had worked his whole adult life after the army, had worked hard and faithful and what he got for that hard work was his brain started retiring before he did. Nothing serious. Medium-level comedy stuff like walking home at the end of a workday. Forgetting he took his car to work, and he needed to take it home again. Arriving, carless, at home about three hours late. That kind of stuff.

Apparently, though, systems analysts for the Department of Agriculture need full faculties. Can't have Idaho spuds suddenly coming up looking like giant strawberries because of a couple of wobbly keystrokes.

So here he is, around and available every day. Cool as cactus juice, like always, but just more available. He lives with us now. That is as it should be. I like it.

We have been pals forever, me and Da. As a young father he was too busy, career building or agriculture networking or whatever, to do a lot of things like teaching his son, my dad, to swim and ride a bike. My gran did all that, and you could tell from the way they were with each other. My dad cried for about two months after peritonitis crept in and squeezed his mother to death.

I never saw my dad and his dad hug.

I hug my dad's dad all the time. Hug my own here and there too, so we're cool. Not the same, though. Not the same at all.

Da taught me to ride: bike, horse, motorcycle, and car. Oh, and glider plane, we did that once. Taught me to cook a little. We've tossed footballs and baseballs back and forth since I was little, but more now that he's retired.

Taught me how to talk, even.

"Keep it lean, Young Man," he always said when I would start running my mouth. "Use exactly the words you need, and no more than that."

"Okay, Old Boy," I said.

Not sure if you would call it jealousy. My dad never got in the way of my closeness to Da, but he was never allover thrilled with it either.

"You know why he does it, don't you, Daniel?" Dad said, chilling the blood right out of me because he was saying it as the two of us stood in front of his mother's open casket.

I couldn't speak. He didn't need me to.

"He does it because of all he didn't do for me. Because of all that *she* did do."

He would know better than me. And there was certainly a lot of sense in what he said. And I still lacked the power of speech. And I wouldn't have spoken up if I could. But there was nothing to stop me thinking what I was thinking, either.

And because he loves me, Dad, I was thinking.

But truth is, Dad and everyone else could be forgiven for thinking I was the only one to ever see any emotion in the old man. Like he saved it up all just for me, and other than that there was nothing inside the Old Boy at all.

"You're doing it again," I say. We are having breakfast together, like we always do now.

"No, I'm not," he says. He goes back to doing it.

"You know what I'm talking about?"

"Do *you* know what you're talking about?"

"Yes, Da."

"Good, then you know what to stop talking about."

What we are and are not talking about is sausages. He used to slice bananas over his cereal all the time. The cereal would vary, the bananas, never. Now he slices sausages, in exactly the same way, as if nothing is any different.

"You know what the doctor said about you and the sausages, Da."

"You know what I say about the doctor and the sausages, Daniel."

"Could you not remind me of that over breakfast?"

"Détente" is what he likes to call this. One side says or does something objectionable, the other side counters with something objectionable, then everyone agrees to just shut up.

"God, is he doing the sausage thing again?" my sister, Lucy, says, walking into the kitchen. Lucy likes to talk as if Da were not here. Da likes to talk as if Lucy were a mentally deficient prostitute. It's kind of a thing in my life, where all the people I really love tend to treat each other abysmally. I choose to see it as a battle royale for my affection.

"In the army I knew a girl named Loose Lucy. She had webbed hands that made a squeaking sound when she would—"

"Da!" I snap. I have heard this one before.

"What?" he pleads. "That story comes with its own limerick and everything."

"Another time, maybe."

"Why do you hate me, Da?" Lucy asks.

"I don't."

He possibly does. Probably not. He says he's nice to her for my sake, because I seem to have some kind of unfathomable warm spot in my heart for the girl. He says it's not his fault that the niceness in question always happens when I'm out.

"Prove it, then," she says, open palm extended.

You might think this does nothing but reinforce my grandfather's venal view of my sister and probably of humankind. But what it really does is please the Old Boy with the notion that his lessons, his hard-won, firmly held life beliefs, have been acknowledged by the youngers. It's their one really good party trick together.

"Love is not money . . . ," Da says, forking over a bill, then another, while parroting his own oft-stated wisdom.

"But money is love," Lucy says, delivering nicely.

"Didn't Ben Franklin say that?" I ask.

Lucy waves her money victoriously in the air. Then she slaps me in the forehead before she passes out the back door, distant as she pleases, aloof, certain, and I ask myself yet again, how could anyone not love Lucy?

"Successful," Da says, turning in her direction, watching her vapor trail as if she has left cunning floating in her wake, "at whatever she does. That girl is going to be just great."

"Maybe you should tell her that every once in a while."

"And undo all my hard work there? Not a chance."

He takes a big spoonful of original Cap'n Crunch, with a sausage disk perched on top. He picks up the newspaper—which is sitting there from yesterday—and starts reading. The paper has clearly been read and reread, crumpled and disordered. Today's is still rolled up on the front porch, if it hasn't been stolen.

Here is what I like about The Condition. It shows how true Da's opinions are, that he is not reacting to mood or weather or a bad night's sleep when he thumps on about the government or sports or idiot businessmen. On the many occasions when he has read to me the highlights of a world that is already twenty-four hours behind us, his words are all but identical to the words he used the first time around. The same venom here, the same disgust there, the same contempt and mockery. These are the moments when Da is stamped indelibly into Da in the way time itself slips into the layers of geology in a mountainside.

Here's what I don't like about The Condition. Every time he repeats verbatim who he was yesterday, he's reminding me how much closer he is to no longer being Da at all.

No unnecessary words, Young Man.

No needless repetition, Old Boy.

"I know, Da, I know," I say, pulling away from the table. "Season's over already. Last team to win the Super Bowl with a backup quarterback was the seventy-two Dolphins. Can't be done."

"Exactly" he says as I actually run down the hall, "and who'd want to be *those* jerks?"

Just like yesterday. Right down to the jerks.

I practically crash through the front door, so anxious to get my hands on today and bring it back for my grandfather to read. I rip the door open, and find the paper's not lying where it's supposed to be.

And it's not stolen either. Not exactly.

"Daniel," Mr. Largs says awkwardly. "Jeez, you startled me."

Da's old workmate, carpooler, whatever, is standing there with our newspaper. He stops in once every few weeks to have a look at the Old Boy. I never could figure out if I liked Mr. Largs or not. Some days yes, some days no.

I don't like surprises at breakfast, though.

"Why are you here?" I ask him.

"I'm not," he says, walking past me when Da barks for him.

It'll be a no-like day, then.

I get Mr. Largs a cup of coffee and a bran muffin. Then sit at the table with the men. Hard to tell why Largs has come by just now, as he doesn't seem to have much to talk about. Mostly he's eating and listening.

Maybe that's because Da is in a talking mood.

"Beer, Largs?" Da asks.

"Cam?" Largs says, startled. Cam was Da's work nickname. "It's only nine thirty, pal?"

"Yes," Da says, all crafty-coot, "but it's afternoon in Europe. Remember the real-beer tour, Largs? Huh? Jeez, we had some fine beers on that trip. All the best local stuff, Daniel. We had Guinness in Dublin, Dinkelacker in Berlin, oh my, and *everything* in Brussels . . ."

You know how you can just tell when someone is looking at you even if you cannot see them? I turn to see Largs snap away from staring at me.

"That wasn't me, Cam," he says coolly.

"Of course it was. We drank Brains in Cardiff! Remember how much we laughed at that? Drinking Brains in Cardiff?" Long, thin smile slashes Da's face.

Sounds like something my grandfather would laugh at.

Largs laughs. "Ah, you mad old hatter. I never went on such a trip."

Da's smile melts, as Largs reaches across the table. He takes hold of Da's wrist, causes him to see the brass bracelet with MEMORY LOSS engraved across it for all the world to see. "We're all getting a little forgetful these days, Cam. I mean, you had the best memory of anyone I ever worked with . . . *ever*. So what chance do I have, huh?" He laughs, alone. "I'm heading to retirement myself in a year or two. Already forgetting left and right."

Da is now staring at the MedicAlert bracelet.

"We drank Maccabee in Tel Aviv," Da says weakly.

"We drank Bud in St. Louis," Largs says, chipper as hell. "*We* were purely domestic, Cam, you know that."

I hate this. I hate this. The memory loss, of course. The low-level unpleasantness that is with us now, because of the conflict of stories? I *hate* this.

Largs knows better. Why does he have to win? Why can't he just fudge and fade his way through a simple stupid exchange, the way people do every day anyway? Why do we need what we're getting here?

Mostly, what is so awful is Da's realization. His unrealization. He knows something is wrong, but he cannot be sure what it is. Like he's fighting somebody in the dark.

Mostly more, even, is that I cannot stand to see him back on his heels. That's it. That's what it is for me. My Da always has the upper hand. Always had it. To see him so clearly *not* in charge is excruciating. And it wouldn't even matter who had the facts straight, because either way, Largs is manhandling him.

It hurts.

"Sorry to rush you," I say to Mr. Largs.

"Huh?" he says.

"We kind of had plans for this morning," I say, standing up to see him out. This is not normally my way. I have been taught respect. I have been taught deference and politeness, often giving these things to people I knew didn't deserve them. I have been taught to treat people *the right way* because, whatever you might be thinking about the person right in front of you, your manners are really offered to the people who taught them to you.

But I was never prepared for having to look out for my almighty Da. I was never prepared for the thought of needing to.

I have not even given Mr. Largs a chance to respond to my words before I am leading him away from my table and toward the exit.

"Okay, then, Cam," says a befuddled Largs, backing out of the kitchen. "I'll stop by again soon."

Da is still examining his bracelet, silent and consumed and possibly unaware he has had a visitor.

"Call first," I say to Largs, on the threshold of impolite, but not over it yet. I hold the door open for him.

Da is looking up at me when I re-enter the kitchen. He has his hand open, palm up, gesturing toward the mysterious piece of jewelry on his wrist.

"It's because of your memory, Da," I say. And because I always relished the challenge of making him laugh, and the thrill when I succeeded, I add, "Your memory, Old Boy, remember your memory?"

For a flickering few, he looks even more perplexed than before. Then he crinkles me a smile.

"I remember, Young Man," he says, and I can see that for now, he does.

It is a funny thing, one that I wrestle with every day now, the notion that he is required to remember that he forgets. A big cosmic joke, that one.

"Did you say we had plans?" Da asks me.

"I did," I say.

"What plans were those, Young Man?"

He has always called me Young Man. Just not this frequently. He never forgets Young Man.

"The races of course, Old Boy."

"The races."

"The horses."

Da loves the horses. I love the horses with him.

"The horses. Today?"

"First race goes off at twelve fifteen, Da. We need to get cracking if we are going to do this the right way. Right? The racing form, the grandstand . . ."

"And the first of the day," he says, beaming, finishing our standard statement of purpose.

"The Triple Crown of earthly pleasure on a sunny day," I say, pointing at the author of the phrase, him.

A horse, a beer, my grandfather, and a full race card. That to me is an embarrassment of riches. The fact that since I'm not strictly old enough and Da has to smuggle me the beer only adds to the fun. So much so that when my folks offered to throw a party for my high school graduation a month ago, I thanked them politely and opted instead to spend the evening after the ceremony at the track with the Old Boy.

I promised myself, anyway. With this being my last summer home before college in September. With this summer being different, in every way, practically every day, regarding Da. I promised myself we were going to be together just as much as I could manage it.

We are going together. This summer, the last summer. Everywhere, together.

He loves *stuff*. He's never been a big drinker, but he *loves* a beer. He loves the sweaty musculature of a racehorse. He loves the awful smell of the race-day crowd that can make even the horses wince. He loves experience, and to be with him when he's at it is to be splashed with all the overspill of his spirit.

He is a human great-day-out, my Da.

In a few minutes he is back from his room and all zipped up in his racing colors. Though they are not all that colorful. His pea-green tweed flattop cap, almost-matching baggy pants, button-down white shirt, gray jacket with lots of pockets—like a fishing vest with arms.

Still, he manages to look dapper as hell.

We are off to the races.

The sun is brilliant, and we are settled into the bleachers with a beer between us and a likewise shared racing form.

How it usually works, especially in fine weather, is that one of us does the reading while the other does the sipping and staring at the sky, the track, the birds, the other customers. Then we switch. Great system.

Only, as the sun warms my eyelids and the seagulls squawk for me to go order some French fries, I realize nobody is reading and filling me in on the day's possible winners.

"What are you doing, Da?" I ask when I open my eyes and find him hunched forward, looking at the concrete step beneath our feet. His elbows are resting on his knees, the racing form resting on the ground.

He looks to me, the flattop cap perched at the precise slight angle, more like a beret, that he always prefers. He is showing me a puzzled face that is almost as puzzling to me. "What do you want me to do, Young Man?"

I point down at the form. "I want you to read me that, like you always do, so we can pick some winners."

His eyes clarify, and focus, like they are mechanical eyes, like they are binocular eyes. "You don't need me," he says firmly.

Not crazy about the tone, so I change it.

"Of course I need you, Old Boy," I say, bumping him playfully with my shoulder. Then I bend down and retrieve the racing form. "Always have, always will."

I am stunned when I feel the grip on my arm. It is not the grip of your average old man. He lifts me right back up and brings my face close to his.

"You do not need me, Daniel," he says. "You *need* to not *need* anybody. Do you understand me?"

The three seconds I waste being speechless convinces him that I do not understand.

"Needing people is death. Needing, is death. Once you have a need, you have a flaw, you have a weakness. Once you have a weakness, you have a bull's-eye. You attract all the wrong kind of attention from the wrong people. Do you understand that?" He still grips my arm. "Do you understand? I might love you—not saying I do, but I might—but I don't *need* you. Nor anyone else." He says those last two sentences oddly loud, like he's putting on a show for somebody. Though there is not another bettor within at least six rows of us, and their body language pretty clearly indicates they could not care less about an old guy and his grandson unless one was going to be riding the other in the third race.

"I understand," I say.

He lets go, takes the beer, and relaxes back in his seat.

"Harry Horse," I say after a few more quiet minutes. Da

has had his eyes closed, so I know he is appreciating the surroundings like he should. I expect things to slip into place now for our grand day.

"What?" he asks.

"I have a horse here, in the first race. His name is Harry Horse. He's thirty-three to one, but he's placed in his last three races and he loves the dry conditions. This sounds really promising."

He tips his cap back on his head. "Harry Horse?"

"Yes, sir."

"That sounds like a horse you would have picked when you were six. Do you remember, when you were little, I'd let you pick one for me out of the paper and I'd bet on him?" He smiles broadly at the memory. "Remember that?"

"Remember it? I loved it. I lived for it. Never won a nickel, though."

"That's because I never went for your foolish picks then, either. Come, let's go down to the paddock."

He hops to his feet, springy and frisky as a colt, and starts bopping his way down the grandstand toward the little parading ground where everyone gets a pre-race glimpse of the big, beautiful athletes.

"Hey," I call, running after him, "are you saying . . . you never bet on those horses for me?"

"Don't be silly," he says, not even glancing back at me. "Nobody in his right mind lets a child bet on a horse." I can tell by the sudden hunch of his shoulders, he is having a nice little chuckle for himself over this.

"Hey. Hello, hey, Da, this is my childhood, my cherished memory you are toying with here . . ."

He stops and waits for me to catch up. As soon as I do, he starts jabbing me in the chest with his index finger. "You are not a child now, though, are you? It is time for you to get grown up. It really is."

He is not poking me hard and in fact is not speaking harshly or meanly. Despite the words, the overall effect somehow manages to be warm.

Doesn't keep me from feeling sorry for myself, or for my younger self, just the same.

"Oh, come on, now," he says, grabbing me in a semiheadlock and walking me along. He would want no part of the moping. As his arm drapes around my neck, over my chest, his MedicAlert bracelet slips down his wrist. I see him look at it for several seconds as we walk.

I want no part of that.

"I still can't believe you tricked me over the bets all those times, Da."

That pulls him away from the bracelet. "What, you were just a kid. You didn't need the money. What you needed was to know that your beloved grandfather was thinking of you and doing something nice for you, even when he was out having fun with his pals. Now that's devotion."

"But you never even did the nice thing!"

"But you didn't know that! That's what was so nice about it. And it shouldn't offend you if a poor little old man saved a couple of bucks at the same time, right?"

"At no time were you a *poor little old man*. Ever."

He laughs, pushes me sideways. "No harm, no foul. I looked good, you felt special . . ."

"A total win-win, huh?"

"Exactly. Cause if I betted on all those stupid glue-pots you chose, it would have been lose-lose. *Mrs. Musby* . . . *Cotton Candy* . . . *Fuster Buster* . . . what kind of numpty bets on horses with names like that?"

He does this trick too—making a fool of his memory-loss bracelet.

"You still remember the names I picked," I say admiringly.

"Course I do," he says. "You're my boy."

"But you never bet on them!" I shout, mock furious.

"Exactly!" he shouts, unmock delighted.

We are approaching the paddock, where the early runners are already doing their beauty parade.

"You are a mean old boy, Old Boy," I say.

He walks a little quicker toward the horses. "You have no idea, Young Man."

I am always shocked all over again when I see horses— especially racehorses—up close. Their polished muscles put on a show all their own as the horses just walk along, unaware of how gorgeous they are. From the way Da stares, ogles, smiles as he leans a bit too far over the rail, I don't think he has ever lost that sensation either.

"You know, in the Middle East, Saudi Arabia, Dubai, they treat horse racing as something almost sacred. When I was there, the conditions I saw, the quality of the facilities, the level of attention to the welfare of the horses . . . you should be so fortunate as to live under those conditions."

I lightly slap his shoulder with the back of my hand. "I never knew you were in the Middle East. When was that? What brought you there?"

"Oh, I was there several times. Glorious places. The

corporation sent me. Business, but pleasure. Pleasurable business."

I look at him looking at the horses. Still wearing that happy grin that makes him look younger than me. I lean out as far as him, to catch his eye and have him look at me. He looks.

"Da, didn't Mr. Largs say you guys only worked domestic?"

"I don't know," he says, looking back at the horses again, smiling again. "Did he?"

I reach across and with thumb and middle finger, pull gently on his MEMORY LOSS bracelet. He stares at it. "Maybe you are remembering it all exactly right."

"I remember," he says.

"So Mr. Largs is lying?"

He turns to face me again, his eyes close to mine.

"Mr. Largs is lying," he says. No smile.

I get a chill.

"There's your horse," Da says, pointing to the beautiful beast wearing the green and white silks.

"You're going to place a bet on him for me. I'd say you owe me. I'm right here now too, so I can see you."

He laughs, pushes back from the rail. "I guess I'm caught. Come on, Young Man, let's go see a man about a horse."

There are a number of different betting booths lined up across the asphalt ground between the stands and the track. They continually flash new odds on each horse, mostly better odds than the ones at the big, official stands inside. It is fun to think of our little bets pushing the odds one way or the other, and while that may not be exactly what is happening, I do enjoy watching the small electronic boards above the booths change while Da places his bets. I lean back on the railing behind me, sip at beer, let the sun warm my smile.

"Daniel," comes the voice from over my shoulder. "Danny boy, how are you doing?"

I don't completely turn, because I never completely turn away from my Da lately. I do a sideways quarter turn to look behind me and ahead at the same time, like a reptile. You can learn to do this, if it is really important.

"Zeke?" I say. "Well, how are you? This is a real surprise and a coincidence."

I am doing that awkward reach-up-and-back handshake with Zeke, wondering why certain types of older guys seem to *have* to shake a younger guy too hard and all over the place.

"Yes," he says, "so great to see you. It's been a dog's age. And your granddad too . . . what a treat. I'm glad I played a little hooky today."

Zeke is the one friend and workmate of Da's I ever saw on anything like a regular basis. He's probably a year or two older, even, and I thought he was retired by now as well. I always liked Zeke, and it was obvious Da thought a lot of him too. We haven't seen him at all since the retirement.

"So, this what the old boy is doing with his days now? I'm jealous," Zeke says.

"No," I say, "we're really not here much at—"

I stop myself when Da turns away from the betting and doesn't see me. I see what comes all over his face when he recognizes no face. Absence, comes all over his face and he toddles cluelessly away.

"Excuse me, Zeke," I say, and bolt.

When I catch up to him, he is staring at his betting slips, staring down at them and still walking forward, bumping and bouncing off people as if he does not know it is happening. I grab his arm. "Hey, you," I say, making light, making fun where there is none.

He looks up at me with that brief horror that is his lost face and I swear I want to slap that face right off him. He stares back down at the slips and then back up at me as if somewhere in there is the correspondence of my face to that ticket. That somewhere in there is the answer and the expla- nation that will pull it together.

And what do you know, he does find an answer in there after all.

"If I were you," he whispers after the last check of the ticket, "I'd kill me."

First thing I do is, I shudder. The full xylophone thing right down my spine and back up again. Then I shout at him. It is not a shout full of reason. "Hey," I yell at him with my scold- ingest tone but little else. He stares. "Hey, Da," I reiterate just in case he missed it the first time.

"Hey," Zeke says, right over my shoulder to Da.

He startles me, and I turn on him now. "Do you mind?" I ask, feeling somehow like I am sheltering my grandfather from something. Much as I have always liked Zeke, I am also aware how he can be an unsettling sort of presence if you aren't prepared for him. He's tall and angular, always in a light gray suit and with skin and hair all the same gray color. He looks, regardless of the conditions, indoor and out, as if he's standing right under harsh fluorescent lighting.

"Ezekiel!" Da says, and my authority and irritation blow

away on the breeze. "Darius!" Zeke says, and they both brush me aside and embrace.

I am the kid here, and that is that.

We are sitting in the stands, up high enough to see well but also to bask in the sun. The first race is a couple of minutes off, and I stare at my ticket, Harry Horse to place. The old colleagues are catching up, chatting about people I know mostly by nickname—Mackie, Doctor J, the Moleskinner—and making very little sense to me. It all sounds boring enough that I think I'll go down and have an encouraging talk with Harry Horse, until there is a slight turn to the conversation.

"Have you seen any of the guys, Darius? From the old team?"

"Not a one," says Da with the conviction of somebody who has no idea.

"Nobody?" Zeke asks. He sounds simultaneously shocked and unsurprised. He throws me a look when I stare at his previous look.

"No, the rats," Da continues. "Zekie, you are the first of the whole crowd. Not even a phone call." There is a pause that one would call uncomfortable, if one liked to really understate things.

"Oh," Zeke says, looking slicingly in my direction for some reason I cannot work out.

"Ah," Da says, at the same time the trumpetty announcer calls out over the PA system that the horses are lining up. "Just that one guy. You know the guy, the putz. Never liked him. Came by, I don't even know why . . . a week ago, maybe two weeks? The guy they sent with me on the Europe trip that time. Couldn't hold his beer for beans."

"Annnnd . . . they're . . . off!" the announcer calls.

And Da is off, along with pretty much every other spectator in the place.

I do love the horses, just like Da does. To hear and feel the thump of their hooves in the turf, even halfway around the track and halfway up the stands, is to feel one of the special somethings of life. You cannot help but get it if you have working senses at all. It draws Da helplessly toward it, and when a lady stands up in front of him, he silently takes an empty seat on the bench in front of us. He's too much of a gent to ever complain to a lady who's enjoying the horses like that.

"Danny," Zeke says right into my ear.

I turn away from the action to see him looking at me, hard and gray. He appears to have no great interest in horse racing.

"People don't usually call me Danny anymore," I say, to be firm with him. I feel like I need to be firm with him, and large.

"Daniel," he says, "your granddad is not doing so well, huh?"

"He is doing fine, thanks."

I turn back toward the race, where it is already apparent that Harry Horse has better things to do than try to run faster than the other horses. Still, it's thrilling.

"Does he talk a lot of crazy?" Zeke asks me.

"As a matter of fact," I say without looking at him, "my grandfather doesn't talk any crazy at all. He gets tired. He forgets. Otherwise, he is sharper than me. Here, look," I say, showing him my ticket and my selection of no-hurry Harry.

"Listen to me, son. I love this man. Probably more even than you do—"

"No," I snap.

Da looks over his shoulder, grinning broadly at me. "I know, he's terrible. Who bets on a horse named Harry anyway? Horse actually looks like he's laughing."

"He's laughing at me, Da," I say, patting his shoulder.

He slaps my knee. "You are a good kid anyway, Young Man."

"Stop gloating, Old Boy, and watch the finish."

He hoots as he does just that, and somehow we are managing to have fun even with Zeke here trying to bleed the sunshine right out of the day. I don't know which horse is Da's, but judging from his mad, hat-throwing celebration, I think he won.

As that happens, something very different happens between Zeke and me.

"Let me tell you just this one thing, Danny—and I am going to call you Danny because I want to talk to that beautiful kid who always showed respect and decency to *this* fine man right in front of us. He does talk some crazy. And when he does, you need to encourage him to talk about something else. I love this guy here and that means by extension I love you, too. So with whatever time you have left with your Da, talk about family, talk about sports, talk about girls and food and flying pigs and music and whatever else passes the time. But if he talks about his work, steer him away."

Zeke gives my neck a small squeeze, both friendly and frightening.

"I am not even supposed to be here," he says. "I won't do this again. Understand? I shouldn't even have come. This is a personal, friend visit. If you see me again, it's going to be business. I am here out of courtesy, and I shouldn't even be."

And the impulse returns, protective, defensive, angry, whatever, but it doesn't feel exactly smart.

"So, then, go," I say.

And you know what? He does. He does what I say, and he goes, slipping away in the post-race mayhem, while the Old Boy fusses around the floor for his hat.

Da pops up, hat on head, ticket in hand. He looks around like he knows something is not right, something is missing, but he cannot quite figure out what.

Winners and losers—and there is no mistaking which is which here—begin making their way down the sunny concrete steps, toward the collection windows, the betting windows, the bars, and the bathrooms, all loading up to shoot the same shots again on the next race and then the next one.

"Whatcha win, Da?" I ask, hand on his shoulder as we bump along down.

He hands me over his ticket and I look at it and we both look up at the results board.

My horse beat his horse. And everybody else's horse beat my horse. My grandfather may realize this, and he may not.

"Will we go for it again, Old Boy?"

"Let us go for it again, Young Man."

He straightens his flat cap, and we go for it again.

TWO

Shut up, Da said.

He never liked to say that, or to hear it. It meant he was furious.

Shut up.

I didn't even say anything, I said.

It was my fault. I was not supposed to leave him. Alone. I was never supposed to leave him alone.

It gets really hard, though. Sometimes. He was sleeping. He slept pretty regular, and so I knew. Approximately. I could go around the corner, breathe some air, think some thoughts. Get a chicken burger. Just around the corner. Just.

Shut up, he said again.

Why, Da?

Shut *up*, Darius, is what he said. To *me*.

Who, Da? Who said shut up to you?

Little puke. That little, little puke.

Who's the puke, Da?

Largs. Little puke Largs. And Zeke. Me, shut up?

When did they tell you to shut up?

Where were you, Young Man?

I am sorry, Da. Really.

Do I smell chicken?

Da? When did they tell you to shut up?

Right there. Up there. On the landing.

The landing. Halfway up the stairs? That landing? Our landing? In our house?

I got a little lost.

What were you doing on the landing, Da? I left you on the couch.

His face. The crumpled face. The don't-know face, but knowing that not knowing is really bad. Knowing enough to be humiliated about not knowing. That face.

Were you going up or coming down when they came to you?

That face. That diabolical sad face.

Lots of people did that, though. My own dad did it. Pause on the landing, trying to remember what he is after. Common.

But not knowing whether you were halfway up or halfway down. That is different. That is way-bad different.

I was lost, Young Man.

And they came and found you. Zeke. And Largs the puke. They came and found you.

Where were you, Daniel?

So sorry, Da, so sorry. Will not happen again. I will not leave you again.

And I never did. Until I was told. I never did again. I could say that at least.

So they found you, on the landing, when you were lost.

Just shut up, for crying out loud, Darius. Just keep your mouth shut.

How did they know you were lost?

Because I said so. I said I am lost. And I said, Daniel? I said, Daniel . . .

I could have cried, I could have. He would have punched me dead in the face, which would have helped.

I am sorry, Da.

You didn't come.

I am sorry. I am sorry.

So they came.

How did they hear you? How did they know to come?

You mean when you didn't come?

Yes. Da. I mean that. Yes.

People can hear, Daniel. Don't be silly. People can hear, easy. Except you, I suppose.

God. I am sorry, Da. I swear, I will never not hear you again. Never.

THREE

I love the prerain weather. It is my favorite weather of all. If it were just always on the verge of raining, and then never actually raining, I would be the most contented guy. The roll-in of the clouds is to me an exciting event, that small breeze, the slightly wet smell of the air. I just love it.

My father does not agree.

"Let's just forget it," he says, all tense as the signs start pointing that way.

We probably won't forget it. Because we have an agenda. This summer, we all seem to have an agenda that nobody talks about. It has something to do with me leaving for college. It has unmistakably got something to do with my grandfather as well. There is a *last time* feeling to almost everything we do now, whether that is true or not.

So Dad has made more family outing plans this summer

than all of the previous ten summers combined. Today's big plan is to go to the antique auto rally, outdoors up at the Governor's Mansion. The governor doesn't live there, but one did at one time, and based on the size of the place, and the grounds and the number of classic cars that were his when he was alive, the man governed more operations than were strictly legal, in my view.

But that does not matter. What matters right now is that it looks like rain.

"Why would we want to forget it?" Mom says, standing in the living room doorway with one of the *three* picnic baskets she has been working on for the last forty-eight hours. She does gold-medal picnic, my mom.

Dad, on the couch, leans straight backward to look through the lacy curtains. "Because, look," Dad says without even gesturing. He could be asking her to confirm that he has swollen glands. She knows him better.

"Come on, Scott, we are not snowmen, we won't melt. We can survive the afternoon even if there is a little bit of rain. It'll be a great day."

"It won't be a great day," Lucy says, swishing into the room with another full basket, plunking down beside Dad, "but it will be pretty all right."

"Sure, Dad," I say.

Da is not down the hall yet from his marathon morning grooming, but he would more than agree. He is showering, shaving, sprucing, doing the still thickish regions of his hair up with his beloved "hair tonic," and whistling his trademark happy tune. For whatever reason, the theme song from *The Deer Hunter* has always meant high spirits for him.

"Hear that?" Mom says, pointing in Da's perfumed direction.

"I hear it," Dad says with resignation.

Dad doesn't love the cars thing, and to the untrained eye it is not even all that obvious that he loves his father (my guess is he does), but one thing is beyond dispute, his father loves, loves, *loves* the car thing.

"Tallyho," Da says, stepping up right behind Mom, as if he has really surprised her. With his scent, he couldn't have surprised her if we chloroformed her first, but never mind.

This does make Dad a little bit happy, because of his agenda. He badly wants to achieve something with these days, even if it can be hard to tell what.

"Reminds me of the old, old days, Pop," my dad says to his dad.

"We never missed the classic car show at the mansion."

"We never did," Dad says.

"And you always argued with me when we got home, right in this room, every time, about which car was the best car in the world. Remember? Jeez. Remember?"

"If these walls could talk, huh?" I say, trying to fit in somewhere.

"Then I'd have to kill the walls," Da says.

Things go a little quiet.

We go to the mansion.

It never gets past a little light mistiness, and really the day is almost perfect for a picnic and a stroll. A stroll across beautiful lawns, around a handsome, stately home, around a collection of the finest machines ever built, and above all, a stroll around a bit of family life and history.

"How old was I, Pop, when you first took me to this show?"

Dad asks as we weave along the row of Studebakers and Pierce-Arrows parked on the great rolling lawn.

"Not too sure," Da says, watching the cars closely, stroking his chin as if the answer is in the bodywork. "Six or eight, I suppose?"

"It was the first big thing we did together, I remember that. I sure remember that."

Awkward. That is what I remember about these two most of all. Always awkward. I never have any trouble getting along with either of them, but boy, whenever we are all together we are one gimpy vehicle, one wheel short or one too many.

Dad is trying, though. For his own reasons, he is putting his shoulder into it this time.

Can't really say the same for Da.

"Don't know why everybody finds the fifty-seven Chevy so special," Da snarls, walking straight away from his son and toward the offending car. "The fifty-five was better."

Dad stands motionless in front of the Studebaker Lark he thought they were bonding over, and watches his old man's back.

"He gets distracted pretty easily," I say.

"He does," Dad says with no emotion. We follow after Da.

"You're right," Dad says when we catch up. "And I remember you always said the same thing, remember, about the Thunderbird and the Corvette. Oh, the 'Vette used to drive you to distraction. Remember that, Pop?"

"Bugs!" Da says.

"What?" Dad and I both ask.

"Bugs!" Da says, and he means it. He goes stomping up the slope toward the mansion and toward the source of his irritation. "No, mere age does not a classic make. No proper car show that calls itself antique and classic has any business rolling in a bunch of these foolish little Volkswagen . . ."

Dad stands still again, watching his father rant his way up the hill to give one of the remaining pieces of his mind to three perfectly innocent little cars.

Dad's face, not normally the most expressive contraption, is drained and defeated.

"You know how he is, with The Condition," I say.

He stares some more.

"He comes and goes," I say. "Does it with everybody."

Dad works up a small, sharp, sad smile for me.

"Not at all, Danny. This is memory lane. The auto show with Pop was always just like this." He pats me on the shoulder, heads in the other direction. "I'm going back with the girls. Keep an eye on him, and come on back when you get hungry."

Just like old times.

"Come on, Dad, don't go," I say, though honestly I'm not all that bothered. They are a handful together, and will never get it right. But still, we should be able to manage better than this.

"I'll see you in a bit," Dad says, and he doesn't sound mopey, so okay. "Go watch him before he does something antisocial."

He means nuts. Whenever he wants to use a more accurate term for his father—mental, demented, loony tunes—he says antisocial instead. I interpret that gesture as love. I do.

"Da," I call as I see him climb into the driver's seat of an old sea-foam-green fat convertible. All the signs clearly state not to get into the cars. The iffy weather has made the already quiet event very sparsely populated today. It's here for three days, and most people are holding out for tomorrow's promised sunshine. So there is no uproar when Da bends the rules, and the nearest plaid-jacketed old guard is probably off having his cucumber-sandwich break. They lean a bit heavily on the honor system here at the mansion.

"Da, you cannot do this," I say, standing at the driver's door like I am a carhop from the days when this car was new, waiting to take his order. He feels it as well.

"Give me a double cheeseburger and a root beer float, sweetheart. And get your skates on."

"Da, come on, they will make us leave if you don't get out of there."

"No, they won't."

He is pulling the very big, green steering wheel this way and that, bouncing in the seat like a little kid. It is a lovable old thing, this car. It's either led a sadly boring life or has been adoringly restored, because it is immaculate. The leatherette upholstery is almost the exact color of the glistening paint job. Big white sidewall tires and lashings of chrome. The white canvas electric top has been retracted to taunt the rain. The two doors are fat. The car is adorably fat.

"'Rambler American,'" I say, reading the raised silvery lettering as I walk around the back.

"Nineteen sixty-two," he says.

"Very good," I say. "You do know your cars. Now come on out, huh?" I am leaning over the passenger door now.

He laughs, stares straight ahead, still juking the wheel as if he's going somewhere. "I do know my cars. And I won't be getting out. Because this is my car."

Uh-oh.

"Please, Da. I mean, you know it isn't your car. What would your car be doing in this show? How could that be?"

"Because they took it off me."

These are the moments when I too want to use those words I should not use. But he is being totally nuts, textbook nuts.

"Who, Da? Who took it off you?"

"They did. And they shouldn't have. Said the car was too distinctive. 'If you're not a shadow, you're a bull's-eye' was the saying then. They had no right. That was too far. That is when it becomes taking the man away from the man, just for the job."

He is trying my patience, and I have got a lot of it. I am sorely tempted, but jeez, he is being certifiably *antisocial* now.

I have to get tough. As tough as I can be with the Old Boy, anyway.

"Old Boy," I say crisply. He looks at me and I tap my wrist, like when you want someone to notice the passage of the time. But I want him to notice something else.

He looks down, and sees his copper MEMORY LOSS bracelet.

He looks back up at me, where I am stupidly making the gesture.

He makes a gesture of his own, at me, also with just one finger.

"Da!" I splutter, and we neither can help laughing.

"Hey!" comes the shout as the dignified old security dude comes ambling up the hill toward us. It has started sprinkling and he most likely was coming up to put the top up, rather than rumbling us. "Get out of there, you."

Da gets tired rather easily these days, so he's always using little energy-conserving tricks. Therefore his finger is still in the air when he gets yelled at by the security guard in the plaid jacket.

Da hates being yelled at, more than anybody else on earth. And he's not too crazy about plaid, either. He aims the finger.

"Right!" the security guard yells, from about twenty yards away. "You two are in serious—"

"Come on," Da says to me brusquely.

"Come on, what?" I say.

The engine starts up, a simple, muffled *brummm*.

"Jeez—," I say, and jump right over the door into the passenger seat as the Old Boy takes off down the lawn, slaloming between T-Birds and Model Ts and JFK Continentals with the suicide doors.

"Da?" I call, just a bit nervously. "Da, how did you start this thing?"

"I told you, Young Man, it is *my* car. Two wires, two fingers, and *varoom*. Couldn't be worrying about keys all the time in those days. I had places to go."

"Holy—," I shout as more mad plaids start appearing and it becomes as much an exercise in not killing people as it is a joy ride.

"Okay, I believe you. Can we stop now? You did your thing, now they will probably be okay if you just give up."

The surprisingly solid old man thwacks me in the chest with his free fist. "That is a reminder, Daniel. *Never* give up. Understand?"

"I understand, okay? Now, just . . . give up."

Thwack.

"Okay, okay."

The plaid brigade have now given up. The dozen or so car buffs milling about seem not to have caught on yet that Da is not an official part of the show. He is pretty classic, after all. He beeps the horn, which is a semicircular chrome bar in the middle of the wheel. Without exception, every customer waves when he does it. He waves back, the straight-up-in-the-air wave that is a must in a convertible. I start doing it too. Feels great.

There are sirens out there somewhere.

"Da?" I ask, and figure that is question enough.

He does not answer, but steers the car toward the innocent picnicking family ahead. They all jump to their feet, stand there staring as we approach.

Da jams on the breaks and manages a sloppy fishtail skid, ruining some nice lawn.

"Coming for the ride?" Da says, like an utterly antisocial, old James Bond.

Lucy comes running.

Da puts out his hand like a stop sign. "Sorry, sweetie," he says. "This is no place for the ladies right now."

The car is a time machine, after all. It's set us back several decades already.

Dad is standing there with his mouth hanging wide-open. A cherry tomato rolls out.

"Coming, boy?" Da asks.

My dad, a boy? Well, I suppose. I suppose. He had to be somebody's boy, at least once-upon-a. But boyish, I can't see. And adventure, I can't see—

He drops his sandwich, runs flat-out in his black picnic shoes, and dives like a stuntman into the backseat.

Da is laughing . . . yes, here I think "like a madman" is entirely appropriate. His son, my father, is floundering around the backseat, his lower half still outside the car because, really, he didn't achieve much speed or airtime in his brave dash. I laugh too, as I turn to see Dad pop up when we officially leave the grounds of the mansion. His hair is blowing forward with the swirling wind, and he looks wildly into my laughter.

"He is stealing a car!" Dad says, making me laugh harder with the sound of it.

"I know," I say.

The sirens appear to be getting louder. Dad looks back over his shoulder at the sound, then at me again. "He's stealing a really *slow* car!"

"I am not stealing anything," Da says, coolly reaching forward and clicking on the radio. Nothing happens.

"It doesn't work," I say. "Too bad, it probably plays all old songs and commercials and nuclear bomb warnings and stuff."

Da just grins wisely. The rain has stopped again.

"What do you mean, you are not stealing? About twenty people just watched you stealing. I am watching you stealing. Why am I even here? I must be . . . antisocial or something."

"Nuts, boy," Da says. "Say it."

"Nuts. Totally, insanely nuts."

"Not at all. You're a good boy and I am glad you came."

Then, like a sudden downpour, Da's mood changes, he stops being silly, starts being . . . something else.

"I owed you this, son. I've owed you this ride for a long time."

He doesn't drive much these days, so under the best of circumstances he'd be a little rusty. Under the circumstances we have, it's pretty hairy stuff. He seems to be fighting the wheel as much as steering it. It's a big thing, like a bicycle wheel, and appears to take a large turn in order to make a small one. So he's all over the wheel, and the car is all over the road.

"Pop," Dad says, "are you sure about this? I mean, I am glad you think you owed me a ride in a nice vintage car and all but—"

Another mood shift. A soft anger comes over Da. "*This* car," he snaps. "This car. *My* car. I owed you a ride in this."

"How is this your car?"

The radio comes on, out of nowhere. It took its sweet time, and it's as if it had this song stuck in its throat since the sixties. Frank Sinatra sings at us that "it was a very good year," and Da's beaming mad, happy expression hints that he agrees.

"How did it do that?" I ask.

"Because it's got tubes in it," Da says, "like an old television set. Takes time for the tubes to heat up." He strokes the dashboard like it's a good, loyal old dog. "You just take all the time in the world, pal," he says.

His foot is all the way to the floor, and old pal is quite obviously going to take its time.

"Pop," Dad says, "how is this your car? That's kind of wild talk."

"Because it is mine. Because I bought it and took care of it and loved it. Until they took it away from me."

"Who—?"

Da takes a sharpish turn, and we all slide sideways with the Rambler's squishy suspension.

"Where are we going?" I ask.

Da answers, sort of.

"Oh, jeez, Pop. Really?"

I look ahead just in time to see the handsome stone-and-steel archway of the cemetery pass overhead.

"We need to make a quick visit," Da says. "She needs to see us men all together, on a day out together. And she needs to see the car. She loved this car and will be very pleased we took it back."

That "we took it" thing has me suddenly getting visions of jail. I look back to Dad, who has sat way back in his seat now and looks a bit shrunken.

I guess we're going visiting. And, from the sound of the sirens, I think we'll be a large visiting party. Hope you are ready for company, Gram.

She looks ready. We drive the car so far up the winding roads of the place, I am sure we are on hallowed, unallowed ground. We pile out of the car and walk over the twenty yards to the grave, silent as monks, solemn as altar boys.

It is the simplest of simple stones. White granite. Dates of birth and death. And

ELLA CAMERON

BELOVED

She was a simple woman in her tastes.

We all stand around her, staring for a minute or so, before Da steps aside like a game show host with a big cheesy smile and a sweeping arm gesture, introducing the car.

"I got it back, Beloved. How's that? How's that?"

"Um," Dad says softly, "the girls, they'll probably be mad with worry about us . . ."

The cops have entered the gates, cut the sirens, and slowly cruise their way up toward us.

"Pop?" Dad asks. "Pop? Are you aware . . . ?"

"Of course I'm aware," Da says. He's still talking to Ella, though. "I am aware, and I am sorry. I said I would get it back, when the time came. I only wish you could have waited. If only you could have waited." He turns to us. "She was a very impatient woman. She was a very feisty, impatient woman."

The cops are standing about eight feet off now, patient and polite, like they are officiating at a funeral rather than hauling in a team of car thieves.

Then, before we even have a chance to say anything, another car pulls up, and it's Zeke.

He steps out of his car and walks right up to Da.

"No finer woman," Zeke says, arm around my grandfather's shoulders.

"None finer," Da says, Dad says.

"No finer *man*," Zeke says, squeezing him harder so that Da's shoulders compress into a small-man frame.

"I'm sorry," Da says again. "I'm sorry."

"Sorry for what, Pop?" Dad asks. "It was just a little confusion, that's all. Nobody's going to—"

"Sorry for . . . everything. Nothing. Never mind. Nothing, sorry for nothing."

It is all coming on fast now, and the confusion is alarmingly visible on my grandfather's face. I step up, like he is mine, like he belongs to me, because these days he does. "Come on, Da," I say, putting an arm around his shoulders and helping him back to . . .

Some stranger's lovely little stolen classic.

I realize what I am doing, and turn to see the two cops, and Dad, and Zeke, but mostly the two cops.

"You don't really have to . . . ," I begin. "You can see what we have here, right? Is it really necessary, since he didn't even realize the car didn't belong to him?"

Dad tries to help. "We got in the car with him to try and talk him down. To see that he didn't maim anybody, but the purpose was to get the car back to the owners just as soon as we could."

"I am the owner," Da says, low and serious as he and I move toward the car again. We stop at the driver's door. "If you want to arrest the car thief, arrest whoever stole it from me." He turns again. "Arrest *him*," he says, pointing to his old colleague and friend Zeke. "He's one of them. He's one of them, took my car away from me. This was only just right. Just getting back what was mine."

This is a very uncomfortable place right now, and a very uncomfortable group. Zeke leans up and whispers a few words in the lead cop's ear. The cops both nod, very understandingly, but what could they possibly understand? I have been right here all along, and I don't understand. Da is living through it, and he doesn't understand. I guess the police simply understand that the old man doesn't *understand*, and that's why they can be so understanding.

"We are going to have to go back to the mansion," says the lead cop, "and see what Mr. Rose wants to do about this. If he wants to press charges, certainly he would be within his rights to do so."

"Rights?" Da spits. "It's my car, not Rose's."

Zeke comes walking toward us, and Da bristles.

"Why are you even here?" Da asks.

"Because I am your friend," Zeke says.

"How did you know we were here?" I ask him. Da is getting so red and puffed in the face, I fear he's going to blow like a bloody tick all over Zeke.

"I was at the auto show when I saw *the show* was becoming my old pal here."

Zeke unwisely does a little chuck move at Da's shoulder. Da slaps the hand away.

"You seem to be lots of places we are," I say.

I see a slash, brief, of tension cross his eyes. "We came to this show together practically every year. We love it. We have always had a lot in common, your granddad and I. Peas in a pod, weren't we, Darius?"

Suddenly, Darius demures.

"Why don't we all go back to the mansion," says the second cop, a larger, younger, more sneery-looking law enforcer. "Something will work out, I'm sure. Why don't you let me have the keys, sir."

"Keys? Junior, I lost the keys sometime around 1967."

Junior smirks, walks over, and leans into the front seat. He looks around the steering column. He pops up, shrugs toward the other officer. "Don't appear to be any keys," he says.

Da walks over, pushes the big cop in a way I never would dare to, and leans in. He runs his hand around a bit under the wheel, wiggles his fingers.

Bruummm.

Da beams. "Just have to be nice to her."

"We are going to all have to go back to the mansion," says the boss cop.

"Right," says the burly one. "I'll drive this."

He tries to sit in the Rambler, and Da gives him a two-forearm blast; if he had a hockey stick he'd be in the penalty box. The cop laughs at him in a way that's both unamused and seriously unamusing.

"Listen," Zeke says, warmly and all too helpfully, "come ride with me, Darius. It'll be like old times."

"No," Da snaps.

"That or the squad car," the big cop says with satisfaction.

"No," Da insists, sure for all the world that he's got choices here.

"Come on, Pop," Dad says, defeat already in his voice. "You don't want to be stuck in a police car. How embarrassing would that be? This will all be sorted out soon if you just—"

"No," Da says.

"What will the girls say?" Dad says, getting visibly distressed over the thought.

"Come *on*." Zeke shows impatience.

"I'm going in *my* car," Da insists.

I look at my father, the man here who I am thinking should be taking charge, taking care, of the old man, of the situation, of me and everything.

And I am thinking, how did he ever get so *weak*? I am sorry for thinking it, and I love the man, I do. But how did the man who had Da for a father become this man?

"Officer," I say, stepping right up to the boss man. "Listen, let us take the car back. Please? You see, right? You see what he's dealing with, his condition. We'll follow you, or you can follow us. . . . He's a good man. He's on the wrong side of the slope now, but he shouldn't have to have it any worse. Please? My Dad will drive the car. Please?"

He stares at me. He hears a lot of stories, of course, a lot of them crap, of course, so this look would be the law-enforcement, I-am-processing look.

Then I do something I would not expect me ever to do. I reach out and squeeze his forearm. With two hands, like I am kneading bread dough. I am a little stunned with what I am doing and a little disgusted too. "He was my granddad," I say.

Cop looks away, looks at Da, looks straight up in the air. "Aw, cripes," he says. Then he pokes me right in the stomach with his finger. "If you guys don't drive straight and very carefully right back to the mansion, I will throw the old guy in jail *and* pistol-whip his grandson."

That worked out better than I expected.

The big cop passes my way as the other one walks away. I think he's going to just slip by but I feel my biceps squeezed like I am getting my blood pressure taken by a boa constrictor.

"My mother has dementia," he says, close, understanding, quietly furious.

I do not know what to say. I do not know what he wants to convey to me or squeeze out of me. I do not get the sense that he quite knows either. But if he does not let go in the next few seconds, I am going to lose this arm.

"I understand," I say, as close to understanding as I can come.

He lets go, just before I produce tears.

The two policemen climb back into the cruiser, and I tell Dad the deal.

"I'm driving this?" Dad says.

"Like hell you are," his dad says.

"Dammit, Darius," Zeke says, "just come with me."

"Listen, Da," I say, "there is no way they are going to let you drive, certainly not before we have sorted the whole thing out back at the mansion. So your choices are: cop cruiser or Zeke or ride in the old—"

"*My* old . . ."

"*Your* old Rambler. As a passenger."

Zeke lets out a small, almost screechy growl down low in his throat, like an animal in a trap. "Darius," he says, and it's pure menace. He gives me a chill.

"This is a family trip, sorry," I say to Zeke as Dad and I link arms with Da. You cannot force my grandfather into anything. But I think we just about managed to charm him.

We climb in and set off, a ways behind the cops, a short distance ahead of Zeke. Dad is driving, and smiling broadly as he comes to grips with the old car.

"I feel like . . . a kid, I guess," Dad says. "Like I am back driving my first car."

"You never drove this machine, fool."

It is a strange combination of stiff and bouncy, but the car has a cool of its own. A frumpy cool, unlike what a convertible usually shows you.

"Neither did you, old-timer," Dad says, actually playing with his father. Strange, stranger, strangest, what is happening here, but bone me if I am going to get anywhere near stopping it. They have had a hard time, these two, for as long as I can remember, and certainly since before that. They both love me, and it shows. They both love each other, and it, dammit, never ever does.

But now.

"I drove it for ages," Da squawks.

"If by ages you mean the time between when you committed grand theft auto and the time the police caught you, then yes, you drove it for ages."

We are just about to exit the cemetery, and Da does what would have been unthinkable before everything became thinkable. He goes for the wheel.

"Pop!" my father screams, and tries to outmuscle the still wiry Da.

"Da!" I shout, trying to get out of my seat belt but not quick enough.

We swerve hard left, over the oldest part of the cemetery, the place with all the famous pre–Civil War graves and even pre-Revolution ones, where all the stones are famously soapstone and ring-fenced and do-not-touch.

Before Dad gets us to a stop, we have touched-up quite a few of them, as well as laying smushed-up waste to their protective fences. I jump out and run to the front to see what the damage is, but the rugged, heavy old frame of the Rambler has done most of the damage, while the dead soldiers are just as dead as before, only now unidentified.

"Pop!" my dad says again, pushing his father away from him and holding him firmly by the arms. The way he would sometimes do to me when he was furious and I needed a shake as well as a talking-to.

No longer full of fight, Da just says, sadly, "*My* car."

Zeke is now standing lordly over the mess of us. "Cripes," he says. "This just got a whole lot more expensive, didn't it?"

We all slump in embarrassed silence.

He's an embarrassment. My mighty, almighty Da has become an embarrassment.

"This was when an automobile dealer treated a man correctly," Da says in the passenger seat, stroking the green, leatherish dashboard. "They had respect. There was respect all over the damn place, and nobody ever talked about it. Not like today. Not like today. The word is everywhere, but that's it. Just the word, "respect" with a whole lot of nothing behind it."

"Okay, no more screwing around," Zeke says, opening the door and helping Da out. The old man puts up no fight. "Gentlemen, it is a good thing this man here is so loved by so many people in so many places. We will sort this out, don't you worry. But I'm going to take Darius to the station myself. Follow right behind, carefully, before we call any more attention to all the havoc."

"Thank you, Zeke, thank you so much. Sure. We will," Dad says, a little weaselly. "Right behind you."

"They would do anything for you," Da says, leaning back over the side of the car, rubbing his hand down the back of the chair, along the top of the half-down passenger window. The window even has its own chrome strip across the top. "They would make buying a new car almost as much fun as driving it," he says, and suddenly snaps the latch on the glove compartment, giggling like a toddler making mischief, before Zeke impatiently tugs him over to his own big, expensive, charmless, boring machine.

I take my seat riding shotgun.

"Dad," I say as he starts weaving around the rubble.

"What, son, I am trying to—"

"Look," I say, gesturing at the open metal flap of the glove compartment.

The compartment door serves as an ancient cup holder, two circles stamped deeply into the metal. Must have passed for fancy a world and a half ago. In between the cups, written in a stylish script, are raised, silver-plated initials: D.C.

"So what?" Dad says. "Daniel, we have to get—"

"Those are Da's initials. Dad? Those are Da's initials. This *was* Da's car after all."

He growls his low and small growl of concentration, fear, anxiety as he concentrates on maneuvering a car that is no sports car, trying pathetically to hang with a car that is a whatever-it-wants-to-be car.

"Don't be so dumb and adventurous, Daniel. It doesn't mean anything. Those are your initials, too, and I don't think this is your car. Is it?"

I look at the side of his face. He has his father's profile, and almost nothing else at all. There is a weird, almost completely new expression there that I am trying to read, can almost read, cannot read.

"It was his car, Dad."

"No it wasn't, Daniel."

Now I can read the expression. It is willful, fearful denial, and I realize I have seen it before.

Hundreds of times.

I shut up.

 FOUR

Tests, they said. Observation, they said.

Why? I said. We already know. We know who he is and what he is and why.

Like hell you do, Da said. He laughed.

Pop, will you please shut up, Dad said.

Don't ever talk to him like that, I said. That was violent. For us. Then. That was violence then.

Understand, son, the man said.

I do not, and I am not, I said. He has been all through this before. You have no test he has not taken.

And failed, Da said. And laughed.

He needs a period of observation, clearly.

He is in the middle of one. Clearly. I observe him. Every day.

It is for the best.

It is for him.

It is for everyone.

It is for the best.

Why are you being so contrary, Daniel?

Contrary Mary, Da said. He laughed.

Why are you being so obstructive, Daniel?

Your acquiescence is not required anyway, son. This is a courtesy.

I am not your son.

No, that is right. You are mine. And I say—

And you're his son, Dad. So why let him go through more unnecessary and unexplained testing when we already know where it all ends up?

Where does it all end up? Da asked. He laughed.

Simple equation, fellas. A brief period of observation on the one hand, a buttload of fines and damages and charges on the other.

Zeke owns the mansion, Da said.

I am a friend of the owner, nothing more.

Observation, Dad said.

Acquiescence, I said. Observation, acquiescence, observation. Acquiescence.

Do not look at me like that, my father said.

That was violence. That was it right there.

Acquiescence, I said.

Observation, said Da. So long, said Da.

FIVE

"Wake up."

"What? No. And tell those birds to shut the hell up too."

"Time for our walk, Da."

He rolls over, just his head, toward his digital alarm clock. He does this amazingly, in my opinion, like his head is a separate entity entirely, or like an owl or a beacon on a lighthouse. Always did that, turning his head that way. He looks at the clock, squints even though the numbers are about seven inches high. Then he shields his eyes with his hands as if he is being blinded by the sun at the same time.

"What time is it, Da?" I ask, standing over him. It is good to keep asking them questions, keeping them as sharp with the basics as possible for as long as possible.

He turns away from the clock, gives me the squinty quizzical look now.

"The numbers are seven inches high for goodness' sake. Are you blind already, Young Man?"

I am never Daniel or Dan or Danny or D.C. or Danny Boy or even District of Columbia, which I loved, not first thing in the morning. That would be too much to ask, and so I don't ask for it. Young Man suits me just fine, as does the attitude. Feisty. We'll actually be needing some feisty.

"What time is it, Old Boy?"

"XL," he says, curling back under the covers like a high school sophomore. At some point, and for no discernible reason, XL became his abbreviation for extremely early. He's rewriting the language by bits now.

"It's time for our walk, Da? Remember, Doc said you were supposed to keep up with it, religious-like. The walking."

He sighs, growls, sits up.

"Doc also says I am supposed to report for *observation* this morning. Quack-ass doctor schmuck."

I splut a laugh out loud at the spit-perfect bratty-boy way he says the word "observation." This is the Da I want.

"Well, walking comes first. Remember he said that? Remember, Da? Remember he said to remember, that every day the walking comes first? Remember?"

These days Da remembers lots of things that never happened, as far as I know. He unremembers lots of stuff that did. Then there is lots more middle ground that who knows whether it did or not, but anyway, I am hoping I can slip some things past him just now.

He grins at me, closes one eye like a pirate, and says, "What are you playing at, boy?"

I make the exact same face. "Not playing at anything. Just

carrying out my duties of care and love for my beloved grandfather. That so bad?"

Among his many advanced skills, my grandfather can *hold* a pirate face.

"What are you playing at?" he says again. "Who walks at this hour? Rats and raccoons, that's who, and that's all."

I sit on the side of the bed. "I'll be the raccoon," I say, poking him.

"The hell you will," he says, slapping my hand aside and shoving me out of his way, "I'm no damn rat."

I didn't lie. We did take a walk. We walked the three hundred yards, in the dark, to the park where we take our daily exercise. At four a.m. it is approximately twelve hours early. Okay, we also take an early walk, to the store about a quarter mile away. But even the early walk doesn't happen until ten, and it is completely negated by being a venture to buy the pack of ciggies Da semisecretly smokes every day. He's not supposed to smoke.

But we don't do our circuits of the lovely, leafy park. We get into the waiting rust-bucket red Subaru wagon belonging to my cousin Jarrod.

"Wa-hey," Jarrod says excitedly as we pile in.

"Wa-hey," Da says, happy to take the backseat.

I get the front. "Jarrod, man, it reeks in here. Four o'clock in the morning, pal, and you are already sparking up?"

He pulls quickly away from the curb. "Danny Boy, I swear, that's from yesterday."

The smoke is clearly still visible in the vehicle's close air.

"I can still see the smoke!"

He bows his head in something like shame. I reach over

and adjust his forehead like it's a rearview mirror. "Watch the road, fool. And pull over. I'm driving."

We make the stop and change-up slick as a slightly addled pit crew at Daytona and are off again.

"I'm really sorry," Jarrod says. "I was just really anxious. I've never been a getaway driver before and I just needed a soother to settle my nerves."

"You are not a getaway driver," I snap.

"Well, not anymore. You are."

"Don't bogart that joint," says Da from the back.

I try to stare back at him while still being safe at the wheel.

"Da!" I say.

"*That* is a cool old man," Jarrod says.

"Da!" I say, suddenly unable not to be the prim parent of the group.

"Oh, please," Da says, waving me off in the mirror.

"He's just being provocative," I say to Jarrod. "Comes with the territory."

"What do you know?" Da says. "For your information, I lived the early seventies almost exclusively on cocaine and fruit smoothies."

Jarrod is laughing and worshipping at the same time. "That's incredible," he says.

"I know," says Da coolly. "Practically nobody had even heard of smoothies then."

They are not related, being from opposite sides of my family. Jarrod is my mother's brother's kid, and for the most part is left alone by the family to do his own thing. He is twenty-seven years old and basically nobody has any clue what his thing might be.

Which is one reason I thought of him.

Another is that I knew he would be available, come on short notice, and not bother with uncomfortable questions.

Best of all, and maybe most shameful for me—if I had time for shame—is that he shares something in common with Da: He will remember very little of what transpires.

I do love him, though. And there's nothing as powerful as the amalgam of love plus need.

"You are sure, Jarrod, that there is nobody there right now. As in no-body, right?"

"Boyo," he says, "the students don't come back for another two weeks, every last faculty and administration type is off squeezing the dregs out of the vacation, and I remain as king and emperor of all I survey there. It's a really small school and all, and I think they even left me with, like, the only set of keys. It's like twenty-five hundred keys or something."

"I have more keys than that," Da crows.

"Really?" Jarrod says.

It's a three-hour drive. I do hope they both get sleepy before they get fussy.

Jarrod is the caretaker at a tiny college that you reach by driving to nowhere and then continuing on for another forty-five minutes. At peak term time it has approximately five hundred students, the vast majority of them sent there for its remoteness. Tuition is relatively high for a small school that isn't known for doing anything particularly noteworthy, particularly well. The truth is, it is a haven for wealthy kids who have slalomed their way down to the bottom of the academic slope. And they do have a ski team. It's a haven for their parents, really, and as such, the place is shiny and handsome and very well-equipped.

And getting in or out, through its private dense woodland covering about the landmass of Rhode Island, takes above-average determination.

"Left at the tree," Jarrod says when I finally prod him awake. We are looking at about fifty million trees.

"Once we find the place, Jarrod, I'm going to kick your ass."

"We're close, we're close, I swear. It's just . . ."

Lots of Jarrod's sentences end just that way, so I am not hopeful.

"Quarter mile up," Da says, surprising me into jerking the wheel. He has not given any sign of consciousness for an hour. "There will be a very small duck pond on your left. A fishing hut and a west-facing bench for watching the sunsets. Fifty yards past that there is a T junction. Take a right. I'm going to kill somebody if I don't get a cigarette."

I quickly get over the mild shock and beyond-mild skepticism I feel about Da's contribution because I don't have a lot of options and it's always possible he is entering that so-far-gone-he's-visionary stage of things. Then when the pond and hut and bench and junction all show up *precisely* on cue, I am converted.

"I don't think that's the way," Jarrod says when I take the appointed right.

"Now go straight for another half mile," Da says. "When you reach the granite quarry, take the small mountain road around the left and you run right into the school."

"There's a quarry?" says Jarrod.

In a short while, we're comin' round the mountain when

suddenly the beautiful private-private school is comin' round right back at us.

"Wow," I say, at the wonder of this place, looking like an Alpine village Heidi might recognize but still having the fresh-minted gleam of something that just went ten years over estimate and ten times over budget.

"Wow," says Jarrod, and he probably has a reason, but right now I don't care what it is.

We all pile out of the red Subaru, and Da is doubled over with arthritis in his hips and back. He walks like a seven for a minute, in a circle, grimacing but working it out.

"Sorry, Da," I say, going to him, working my thumbs into the spots on his back I know too well. The hips are on their own.

"Sorry what? Get me a cigarette," he says irritably.

I grab my backpack out of the car. It is actually a rucksack, fairly roomy, but still not much for the both of us on an open-ended trip. The important thing right now is the sturdy little box in the front pouch.

Da draws in, and in, three inhales before one exhale, and it is as if he is imbibing hinge oil directly into his bones and joints. He straightens up, then up, and up, until he has been pneumatically returned to his full physical self.

He looks at the butt admiringly. "Why on earth do you get such bad press?"

"How do you know this place, Da?" I ask as I wander through the parking lot. Jarrod has wrangled the rucksack over his back and is ambling toward the curved chalet-style building that looks like a hotel and must be the student lodgings. Our lodgings.

"You guys are going to love this," he calls back. "It's just like living in *The Shining*."

"Can't beat that," Da says, lighting another cigarette to make up for the deprivations of the early rise and long drive.

"Da?" I say.

He turns from Jarrod's direction and toward me, slowly taking in the panorama as he does. It is piney, crisp, and fresh, trees looking like they were peed on by dinosaurs, the parking lot empty as advertised, the small words spoken floating easily on the breeze and bouncing back off the woods and unpeopled buildings and stony silent hills like faces of old wise men who will never tell.

He smokes less frantically now, smiles, and flashes me the unmistakable sharp lucidity of the good times.

He is happy. Right now. Unobserved.

I am a good boy.

"An unobserved life, Young Man, is the only life worth living."

"Is that so, Old Boy?"

"Yes. You are not who you are, when you are being watched. You never even find out who you are, while you are being watched."

"Well, I suppose that's why we are here now. To get you away from the *observation*."

"I know."

Everybody everywhere says "I know," I know. It means next to nothing. But when Da says "I know," I need to know.

"Do you, Da? Do you get what this is all about?"

He pauses, walks up to me with his head tilted in a quizzical way, a thin smile aimed at me. When he is right in front of me, he holds up his wrist, showing off his MedicAlert.

"Daniel, this says 'memory loss.' It does not say 'moron.'"

I look down at my feet for a few seconds. It has been my intention right along to be sure I never made him feel like that.

"I'm sorry, Da. I swear I didn't mean that at all."

"Didn't mean what?" he says chirpily to the top of my shamed head.

This is not a good time for one of his mental departures. I look up expecting the sad, scary vacant look.

Except he's grinning, almost giggling like a kid.

"So you were just faking that, yes?" I say.

"I'm always faking," he says slyly. "You really should never pay any attention to me at all."

"Okay," I say. "I won't."

"And one more thing. You are really going to have to toughen up. Don't be so sensitive. Sensitivity is fatal in this world. I wouldn't have cared if I hurt your feelings, so don't worry about mine."

I wait to see if he's got anything else. When he doesn't, I nod and walk past him on the way to the dorms.

"I guess it's a good thing I don't pay attention to you at all now."

"Ha!" he says at my back. It is a very approving ha.

I suppose this could be a dry run for my actual college experience coming up in a few weeks. If it is, I will be well prepared to be part of the oddest dorm trio on any campus.

Jarrod and Da are talking at the table of our small kitchen when I come out from the shower.

"Sheez-o, man, Danny, why didn't you tell me what a full-blown trip your granddad is?"

"I guess we're just modest on this side of the family. Why, what's he been telling you?"

"What *hasn't* he been telling me?"

I wait for elaboration. I wait in vain.

"Da?"

"I've just been filling young Jarrod in on the thrills and chills of my exploits in the world of agribusiness."

"Angry-business," Jarrod pipes up. "That's what the guys all called it."

I stare at Da for signs. Is he in? Is he out? Is he still with us?

His squint-eyed mischief-maker face tells me he is very much in. There is none of the crazy on him right now.

"Okay," I say, taking up a chair opposite my grandfather, "what exploits would those be?"

"Tell him the Tel Aviv one," Jarrod says.

"I believe someone said something about a smoke?" Da says, all cagey hold-back all of a sudden.

"Absolutely," Jarrod says, fishing a Rastafarian-quality spliff out of his shirt pocket.

"Da?" I ask, and I hear myself sounding like a prig, but really. "Are you serious here?"

"Sure, why not? Now that I am *retired*"—he chews every letter before spitting the word out—"I can self-medicate at will. That's what they want anyway, really."

Jarrod lights up, pulls hard, then breathes out the words "Tell Tel Aviv."

"There's not a whole lot to tell, really. I just had an assignment to climb up the front of an apartment building that was partially under construction, climb onto a man's balcony, and damage his eyes."

"What?" I say in a tall, shrill voice. "What? I mean, *what?* You never did that. He's pulling your leg, Jarrod."

Jarrod looks deflated, watching Da draw hard on the smoke. Da then speaks in that smoke voice. "All true," he rasps.

"What? What? Why? Why would you do that?"

"Because I was told to. I was just doing my job. You know, a straightened paper clip punctures straight through a man's eyelids with surprisingly little resistance."

"What?" I am not making much progress, admittedly. "What? What does any of that have to do with *agribusiness?*"

"Angry-business," Jarrod corrects me. "You want a hit off this?"

"No," I squeal. "Come on, Da. Stop with all the nutty now. You are scaring me here."

"Don't be scared, Young Man," he says, and all trace of jokiness has vanished. "Don't be scared. It doesn't do you any good, and it keeps you from realizing your potential."

Potential. It sounds like a funny word at the moment. Could my dear grandfather possibly have the potential to create the grisly mayhem he's talking about? I am not stupid; I am not naive. I always suspected his professional life wasn't quite as tidy and straight as he made it out to be. And yes, the weird special interest he's been getting from old colleagues suggests that things are more serious than I had believed. But I was thinking maybe they were just getting worried that his loose cannonism meant he was going to start disseminating classified-type information. I would not have believed *this*.

And I still don't.

"Why would you actually maim another person, Da? It just doesn't compute. You can be a prickly guy sometimes, but there's no way you could ever be—"

"He was a scientist of some kind," Da says offhandedly. "I really didn't do a lot of homework on him, so I didn't know hardly anything about him. All I knew was that he was doing some great and important work, for which he needed his eyes, and he was doing that work for the incorrect guys."

Now, I get a chill.

I take the joint.

I cough hard enough to break my own ribs, because I don't smoke.

Da hops up and pounds my back, hard and many times, until I have to ask him to stop.

Here is one of my weaknesses, the kind of thing Da always mocked and scolded me for. When events spin out my control and understanding, I instinctively call my sister. Yes, it is childish, and no, she does not normally come up with insights or warm words. In fact, she is usually kind of an ass.

But the world gets back on its axis when I do it. For whatever reason.

I take out my cell phone.

"What are you doing?" Da asks.

"Making a call. Just calling home. To see if anybody even noticed we're gone."

"No," Da says, and wrests the phone out of my hand with such calm authority, I feel, for a second, like that other stuff could actually be true. "No cell phones, Daniel. The basics here. You use your phone and they will be here today. You want them to catch us?" He assaults my phone like he's disemboweling roadkill for supper, removing the battery and stuffing it in one pocket, slipping the SIM card into another.

"Hey, I got that phone for my graduation," I said.

"You're in college now. Stop living in the past."

Again, it's in his words, his tone. It was almost a lark, stealing him away so he could avoid observation. But hearing him actually put words to it, hearing him acknowledge . . . *them* . . . *catch* us . . . makes it feel real and nasty and dangerous.

"Technology is for chumps," Da says.

"This is for real, isn't it?" I say, coming very late to the party.

"Yes it is, Young Man."

"And it's serious."

"Deadly so."

The air is heavy, smoke hanging there like it is never going to leave. The big, fat, scary words floating there too. I am speechless.

Jarrod is not. "Tell another one, Da. What else you got?"

"Okay," says Da, like the genial gramps telling the little ones bedtime tales. "But first we have to eat. I am starving."

The thought of food makes me retch.

There are a lot of woods around this campus. That's a good thing, because woods are good. Comforting, relaxing, healthifying. But it's also a bad thing because I never realized before that woods are damn scary.

In fairness, everything is scary now.

I am seeing shadows behind every tree. I hear unfamiliar bird calls and I am thinking it's *them* and their array of clever spook tricks, tracking us and closing in and surrounding us. A chipmunk darts out of a hole and scares the squat out of me. A chipmunk.

Da looks as comfortable and calm as could be. It may have a little bit to do with the fact that in the last twenty-four hours he has gotten comfortable and calm with Jarrod at least three times. He's not high right now, though. We are taking our daily exercise in a whole new atmospheric landscape, but he has that same contented air about him as if we were walking in the park back home.

It's good to get out with him, just the two of us. I asked Jarrod if he wanted to come and he looked at me as if I had offered him some amateur, unmedicated surgery.

"Why would anybody want to just, like, walk?"

So I just asked for guidance, as he was the caretaker and all. Like, where freaks like us might find a decent walking trail or two.

"What is this, an exam? I am an employee here, not a student."

"Jarrod?"

"Over that way somewhere," he said, pointing vaguely with his nose since his hands and eyes were taken up with butchering a bunch of simulated people on his video game.

So we found "that way somewhere" basically on our own.

"I know you don't like to hear this kind of thing, Da, but I am really worried."

"Don't be," he says, looking all around at the flora and fauna.

"You have to stop saying stuff like that. It's not helpful. This feels like a dangerous situation, and sometimes fear is the correct response to such things. I mean, if you aren't just talking nonsense—*ow, ow, ow, stop it.*"

He has grabbed my wrist, bent it forward, and applied his thumb hard to the depression at the base of my thumb. I am down on one knee before I even realize what's happening.

"I love you, Daniel, more than anyone on earth. And I do not talk nonsense."

"I understand," I say, straining not to spill tears since that would probably provoke him to paper clip my eyeballs out. He helps me up again.

"You okay?" he says.

I nod. "So, what's going to happen now?"

"Well, I'm not going to kill you or anything, if that's what you mean. Unless you make me really mad."

"I won't do that. But I meant—"

"I know what you meant. The answer is . . ."

And here he does something that shocks me and unsettles me probably more than all the other stuff. He takes me by the hand, and holds on as we walk. I stare, in disbelief, at my grandfather's inhumanly cold hand.

"The answer is, they are going to track me down, wherever we go. They will get me and bring me back and, one way or another, shush me."

I shake loose of his hand, as if he has just done something to offend me, though he certainly has not.

"Shush you?"

"Yeah," he says, "shush, you know . . ." He holds an index finger to his lips. "Hey, we had a very funny thing back when I was still working. If somebody needed shushing, we would do the regular shush, with the one finger. *Shhhhhh*. If it got more serious, then we elevated to quadro-shush." He holds up four fingers of one hand like a karate chop and wiggles them in front of his lips as he shushes. "Then, if it was *serious* serious, they got the octo-shush." He holds both hands up now, eight fingers waving like sea grass underwater, in front of his shushing lips.

"That is funny," I say, "I guess."

"Yeah," he says, lowering his hands and looking up high into the tree where some large dusky bird of prey just dropped in. "I'm pretty sure they are going to octo-shush me, Young Man."

I can almost see Da's fade-out coming, happening as if by design, as the cloudiness moves across his face.

"Because of all that stuff you did? What you know?"

"Huh?" he says, looking distractedly at the bird.

"It's because you decided to start talking about it after all this time. Maybe your conscience is trying to make a comeback."

He shakes his head, not entertaining that theory for a second.

"I just forgot to forget." He shrugs.

"Well, just stop talking, Old Boy? Simple. Clam up, for god's sake, and everything can go back to fine and you and I can go to the races and stop *being* the races."

He shrugs again, and it is another new and unwelcome trait. Never a shrugger, this man, never on the fence about anything. "What the hell. I'm dying anyway, aren't I?"

"You are not—"

"It is fatal, and you know it. Even I know it. Takes too long anyway. Disassembles you by bits, till you are nothing *but* bits. Maybe somebody gives me a homemade lobotomy, they're just doing me a favor, sparing me the worst of it."

"Let's go," I say, tugging him by the arm. He has mentioned his coming death only a couple of times but it makes me want to kill him when he does. "You've stared at that bird long enough."

He follows along with no resistance. It feels ever so slightly better to get the small sense of some control of something.

"You are a killer, Daniel."

"Yeah, okay, right," I say. I may sound patronizing, but I may not care.

"You are a killer, and you always have been one. That's why I have always loved you the best."

Me. A killer.

All the familiar words I am not supposed to use on him—demented, crazed, lunatic—are all the words I want to use on him right now.

Instead, I go a different way.

"If I am a killer," I say, turning and confronting him flat-footed, "maybe it's the other way around. Maybe you didn't love me best because I am a killer. Maybe I am a killer *because* you loved me best."

I suppose I expected that to cool his jets. But nothing comes as expected at this point.

As I walk on ahead, he says to my back, "I hope that's true."

It is all changing so quickly, so quickly. It is as if the grandfather I knew, whom I did not know, is a completely alternative version of himself now. We sleep a second night in the utter stillness of the ghostly college, and it is a kind of paradise, a kind of hell.

I wake to every shift in the fabric of the universe. I swear, one time I jump up at the sound of pine needles falling to the ground outside. Da said he slept more soundly last night than he has in memory. Which could mean three days. Still, it sounds good and he does look some kind of refreshed. I think he could probably stay here indefinitely.

Yet we don't have indefinitely. We don't have remotely indefinitely.

It is barely light when I get dressed and go out. I head over to the sports hall, where Jarrod and I went and shot baskets in the echoey gym yesterday during my grandfather's nap. When Jarrod missed and retrieved his twenty-fifth free throw, I wandered off to look over the rest of the building. There was a game room with pinball and darts and foosball. There were vending machines. There was a small gym upstairs. And there was a quaint old-style pay phone booth.

Da confiscated my phone, but there shouldn't be any reason not to use a landline, right?

So that is where I go, when the day breaks, my mind aches . . .

She answers her cell phone after four long rings.

"Lucy?"

"Holy macaroni, doofus, where are you?"

"You can't tell anybody."

"I don't want to tell anybody. I just want to hear it myself. All kinds of everybody are looking for you guys. What have you done, ya gimp?"

"I took him."

"You *took* him? Dan, that is a pretty flat explanation for somebody who just stole an ill and elderly man. What's this phone, anyway? I almost didn't answer when this number came up. Where's your phone?"

"Da took it off me."

The following silence is designed to make me listen to my words over again and feel the fool. I do it. This is what she does.

"So you stole the old man, and the old man overpowered you and stole your phone."

This is the other thing she does really well. She rephrases circumstances and plays them back at you in order to compound your feeling of stupidity.

"Before, I was just a little worried about you. But jeez, Bonnie and Clyde you ain't."

"Right, thanks, Luce, I'm glad I made my one call to you. I feel a lot better now. Talk to you soon."

"Sheesh, you and your thin skin."

"I don't have thin skin. Why do people keep saying that?"

"Maybe because you get all teary when somebody criticizes your new haircut."

"That was not teary, that was hair products stinging my—"

"Where are you, Dan?"

"Entebeyar."

"You are making things up now. There is no such place as Entebeyar."

"No, that was not a name. It's a saying, Da's been using it, about his work days. NTBR. Not to Be Repeated."

"So then the two of you are out there playing secret agents. That's actually very considerate of you, joining up to your grandfather's dementia. Darn sweet."

"I half think I am. It has all gotten so surreal, Lucy."

"Where *are* you, Daniel?"

"Entebeyar."

"All right, already."

"We came to stay with Jarrod. At the college."

There is that silence again.

"*Cousin* Jarrod?"

"Yes."

"You mean, *this* Jarrod?" She makes a sharp-intake-of-air noise, like either she has just sipped scalding soup, or she's imitating Jarrod toking up.

"Yes," I say.

"Brother, I know you haven't been gone long, but it is still a miracle you remain alive."

I take a deep breath, pound the pay phone with coins.

"That's a lot of coins," she says.

"This is a lot of freaky."

And to the best of my ability, I tell her.

"Are you on drugs?" she says after a bit. "Dan, sorry, but all signs point to you being on drugs. There's Jarrod. There's the fantasy stuff, there's the poor judgment in running in the first place, there's the poor judgment in running to Jarrod . . . there's Jarrod . . ."

"I am not on drugs. I am starting to think I am stuck in somebody else's hallucination."

"I still can't believe it," she says. "He was always mean, but I wouldn't think violent or scary to people who were not his family."

"All I can tell you is, somehow, it seems a little more believable all the time now. He is kind of scary."

"Dan, then leave him. Or bring him back. Let them deal with him."

"That's what you would do?"

"Absolutely."

"I can't. I can't. He's . . ."

She knows. Everybody knows. She doesn't feel the same way about him but she feels that I feel it.

"You are a dope, Danny."

"Maybe. Don't tell anybody."

"Everybody already knows you're a dope."

"No, I mean don't tell anybody that you talked to me. Octo-shush."

"What is that, now?"

I explain octo-shush.

"When they catch up to you, you are both going in for observation. You know that, don't you?"

"No. Because they are not catching us. I'll call you."

"Okay. Be careful, Dan. Right? Take care of yourself first. Right?"

"See ya soon."

After I get off the phone with Lucy, I take my slow meander back from the gym. It is a cracker of a late-summer northern feeling. The air is autumn cool, and mist rises everywhere as the sun gets to work, cutting through the trees and landing in shazam slashes over the buildings and grounds. The pine smell is like it's been pumped out of a cypress-size spray can. You really could spend a lot of time here. It would nice to be able to spend a lot of time here.

When I finally reach the dorms, Jarrod is in our kitchen eating a bowl of Froot Loops the size of my head.

"Seen Da yet?" I ask him.

"No, sir, not yet. Froot Loops?"

"Um, maybe not, thanks."

"You sure? You need to get your five-a-day."

The man does make me smile. "You're a good man, Jarrod. Thank you for this."

"You kidding? Pleasure's all mine. I can't wait for the codger to get up so I can listen to him."

I take a seat across from him.

"What's the worst thing he's told you?"

"Worst? None of them are bad. You mean best?"

"Okay, then?"

"My personal favorite was the one where they set a guy's face on fire with his own glasses, in the sun in Cyprus."

It's been a long day already.

"Try not to believe everything he says, Jarrod. He's not well."

"Cyprus is really, really hot, though. And the guy was a nerd, with flaky dry skin and very thick glasses. That's the key to the story, the very, very thick glasses."

He really is a good guy. And it is to everybody's benefit that he located the only job he could likely ever do.

"Anyway, again, thanks. You really helped us out here, and put yourself in a tough position. But we are going to have to get moving soon."

"*Mi casa es su casa* . . . until the students come back. Then the boiler room is *mi casa* and you have to get on out of here."

I head out of the kitchen. "We'll be gone well before that, I'm afraid."

I walk down the hallway to Da's room, just on the other side of the showers from mine. When I get there, the door is open, his bed is empty, and all his clothes are there on the floor.

"Jarrod!" I shout, echoing down every empty hall in the school and chasing all the birds into flight.

SIX

What is violence anyway, he asked.

A punch in the mouth? A cluster bomb? A needle in the eye?

What about just doing nothing when you should be doing something? Sometimes, can that be violence?

Let Gorgons be Gorgons, Da said. Sometimes hurt has to happen, he said, and that is not violence. Sometimes nobody lays a glove, and it's barbaric.

Can you do what you need to do, whatever you need to do, at the moment you need to do it, Young Man? That is the important thing. That is the separator.

Could you do it, if you needed to? Whatever *it* might be?

SEVEN

"Where could he be, after all, Dan-o? It's a small place, a safe place. Couldn't hurt yourself if you tried, and I've tried lots."

"A small place? Jarrod, there must be hundreds of acres here."

"Really?"

It is a tall, tall order, with the grounds being so vast, so densely wooded for much of it. And I don't even feel safe calling out his name, because I am paranoid that somebody who is the wrong somebody is going to hear us.

"Olllllldd duuuude!" Jarrod calls out.

I punch him hard on the arm.

"Shut up," I tell him in an angry whisper, though even I think whispering is more than paranoid.

"Mwaaa, waa, waa," I hear, garbled and possibly not even

words to begin with, but certainly human. The sound seems to come from a long way off.

"There," Jarrod says with some pride. "I found him for you. Calm down and let's go celebrate."

"What are you talking about? We're going to get him."

"All the way down there? On foot?"

"Grrr."

"Come on, we'll go get the tractor-mower. I have to cut the grass down on the playing fields this morning anyway."

"You are so lazy," I say. "Which way exactly? I am going down right now and you can meet me there."

"Well, for me it's up that paved road and then right on the next one, but as the crow flies, probably straight through these bits here. I'll race ya."

I am already cross-country running through the trees before I can answer his dumb challenge. I'm dumb enough myself, trying to call out to my grandfather as I run full tilt, but trying to whisper-yell so as not to be heard by anyone else.

He answers, though. Well, no, he doesn't. He is there all right, probably a couple of hundred feet away at this point, and he is vocalizing, but it isn't to me, and it isn't in any English I recognize.

"Da," I pant as I emerge into the clearing. If it were a football field, I'd be at my own goal line and he'd be at about the opposing thirty-yard line. I defy my unfit body and break into another sprint. He sees me.

And breaks away in the other direction.

"Da," I call out again and again, but he barely looks back at me as he plunges into the far woods.

Eventually, I catch the old guy, and he is panting, but not as hard as I am. I turn him around and we breathe heavily into each other's face. I am sweating a lot, but the cool forest air is peeling off the heat quickly.

It must be cooling him even quicker, because he is standing in his bare feet and pajamas. He has deep scratches on his hands and feet, bleeding like he's been crawling through bramble hedges.

"What are you doing, Old Boy?" I ask, and I feel myself choke up just slightly as I ask it.

I step forward, to hug him, to warm us both, to stop him from answering.

And he punches me dead in the mouth.

I can hear Jarrod's tractor-mower thing coming down the hill as I run after my grandfather once more. I can already feel my right eyetooth wiggling in its socket and a little bit of fat lip and blood.

"Jeez," I say, catching him, wrapping him up, and, dammit, hugging him.

"Kill me, then," he says. "It's about time you caught me. You boys were always two steps behind. Kill me. Fair enough."

"It's not them, Da," I say, holding him tight, breathing close enough into his ear to bite it off. "It's me. It's Daniel."

He does not respond for a full minute. Then, "I was just going for cigarettes."

"Nothing wrong with that," I say. "Nothing wrong with that."

"It's cold," he says.

"Would you like a lift, sir?"

"I would, yes. I would like that. You are a good boy," he says.

"Well, I try to be," I say, releasing him from my grip and steering him back toward the field and to Jarrod. I hold on to his shoulders as if he is manually operated.

When we step back onto the smooth grass and Jarrod steps up to meet us, the old guy acts once more on impulse.

He punches unsuspecting Jarrod straight in the face.

Jarrod actually goes down. But he is laughing as he gets back to his feet. "Wow, that hurt a lot. Spankings from a granddad like you would put kids in the hospital."

We hop on the mower once Da starts recognizing Jarrod's distinctive manner.

"Did you ever kill anybody?" Jarrod says, steering the machine back up toward the dorms.

"Only once," Da says, staring at the surroundings as if it were all just built and planted since he passed through earlier this morning.

"Tell it, man. Tell it, come on."

Da hugs himself through the chill.

"No, I won't," he says. And the chill in his voice is so noticeable that even Jarrod recognizes not to ask again unless he wants to be number two.

"Did you take your medications this morning like you were supposed to?" I ask the shivering, shriveled Old Boy as he slips back into bed.

"I don't take medications. Medications are for gimps, simps, and wimps."

"Oh, another saying from your work?" I ask, snarky.

"I don't have work. I am retired."

"Where are your meds, Da?" I snap, tearing apart his modest

allotment of underwear and toiletries packed nicely in his drawer like a new boarding-school schoolboy.

"I don't have any," he growls.

As he should, growl. Of course he doesn't have his medication. I packed our stuff.

I blew it.

While Da sleeps and Jarrod mows, I pace. I sweat and fret and try and come up with a solution to this because we cannot go back home for the medicine because that will be the end of the road, and we cannot call the doctor to order more because that would give us away as well, and we sure as hell can't go any further at all with *no* medication.

"My feelings exactly," Jarrod says, walking in with grass clippings covering his legs.

"I guess I was thinking out loud," I say.

"I guess you were thinking out loud, out *there*," he says, pointing out the window. "I could hear you outside. I could practically hear you while I still had my headphones on."

I'll have to watch that.

"What's the matter anyway? You got him back. You didn't lose him again, did you?"

"No, I didn't lose him again. But I did something just as stupid. I forgot to bring his medicines. Without those . . ." I shake my head, pace some more, grab two fistfuls of my own hair.

"You are a sight, cousin."

Jarrod watches me as if I am in a pet-shop window. His amusement grows.

"What?" I say.

"I might know somebody."

I freeze. "What do you mean by that?"

"My guy. In the next town. He claims he can get exactly anything I want."

"Don't screw with me here, Jarrod. I am very much on edge."

"I can see that. I'm sure we can hook up something for your problem as well."

"Yeah, one medical emergency at a time," I say. "But thanks, I'll let you know."

We wait it out while Da sleeps off his moderately big adventure. By the time he comes into the kitchen, he looks a bit more rested, settled, and at least is dressed in regular outside attire.

"Where can I get a cigarette?" he asks.

"I know just the place," Jarrod says.

We are off once again in the Subaru, and this time I don't have to drive. There is a slight indication my cousin is starting to get the hang of low-level responsibility and commitment to a task.

"This is great timing," he says. "I was fresh out of my own medication and had to make this run today myself."

Close enough.

"Are we getting medication?" Da says from the back. "For me, too?"

He sounds so weak and lost to me, I want to cover my ears. I want to promise him anything. I want to make him better with my own stupid hands. I turn, see him wringing his own hands feverishly. "Would you like some, Old Boy?"

"I think maybe I need some. I don't feel well."

"We'll take care of you, Da. Just sit back and watch the scenery."

He does, and the scenery does basically the same granite-trees-granite-trees-flying-by trick for the whole forty-minute ride.

"Are we there yet?" asks a convincingly bored-out-of-his-skull voice. It belongs to Jarrod.

"You are the driver," I point out. "You tell us."

"Just about there," he says as we finally turn off the highway and onto the lead-in road to the town. Five minutes later we are pulling into one of those classic northern New England towns that *never* wind up on postcards. There is a small steel-colored river running past a couple of hulking and empty factories that must have made shoes or shoelaces or shoehorns or something that somebody else makes even better now. The river has a couple of bridges over it, but neither is covered like in the calendars. They should cover them. They should cover everything else while they are at it.

"Oh yeah," I say, admiring the ambience.

"You want meds or don't ya? Don't be so snooty."

"Oh yeah," Da says, recognizing something else. "Bet this town arms more militias in a year than I ever did. And I spent a lot of time in Angola."

Like in slow motion, Jarrod and I turn to Da, who is poker-faced.

A horn wails at us. I spin and yank the wheel, pulling us out of oncoming traffic. The other driver is wailing even louder.

"Lucky you didn't kill us," I shout at Jarrod, shoving his head sideways.

"Even luckier that guy didn't," Da says, staring out the back at the other driver, still menacing us with a finger.

We pass several vehicles as we negotiate the main drag, and they all look like they were monster trucks in their playing days. Then we turn off the road, off that road, and then off that one. We park at a modest-looking little shop that appears like it doesn't want to bother anyone. VENUS EXOTICS, it says in red lettering on a cream-painted window.

"Is this what I think it is?" I ask as Jarrod leads us in.

"Not if you think it's a bakery," he says.

"Whoa," I say as we head straight down the middle of three aisles. The woman behind the counter, dressed in a schoolgirl uniform, waves us through to the back. If that is her uniform, she's kept it nice for about forty years.

Da keeps muttering behind me as we walk toward the door that says MANAGER. I pull him in front of me and guide him. "Whoa," he says. "Wow."

"Jarrod," the man says when we walk into the office.

They shake hands. Da and I get introduced.

"Nice place you've got here," Da says.

"Thank you," the man, Matt, says.

"I have never seen so many giant rubber penises in one place in my life," Da marvels.

"Please," Matt says, "you're making me blush."

We have only just met, but I am guessing that is purely impossible to do.

"Anyway . . . ," I say, catching Jarrod's eye.

"Yeah, Matt," Jarrod says. "About business."

"Right, right, I've got your order. I take it your friends are here for something as well. What can we do?"

This is where it gets complicated.

I can just about recall the main couple of medications Da takes daily to almost hold it together. Matt is something of an expert, but he is not 100 percent certain.

"Do you sell cigarettes?" Da asks politely. His hands are starting to tremble from a number of different deprivations.

"Sorry, sir, I do not."

Something my grandfather always pounded into me, and I always believed it anyway, but now that I am seeing his hard side I am believing it fantastically: Manners beget manners. Don't start a ruck when you can just say please and get the same result. I suppose it works with a sex-shop black marketeer as well as it does with anybody else.

"Here," Matt says, sliding a nearly full pack of Camels across his desk.

"You're a good man," Da says, smiling pleasantly.

"Keep that to yourself," Matt says, smiling likewise.

"Entebeyar," Dad says.

"Huh?" Matt says.

I must break in. "Listen, we have a time thing here. You might not be one hundred percent sure about the medication, but it sounds like the stuff to me. And we are one hundred percent desperate, so we are going to go with your sense on this."

"How old are you?" Matt says.

"Eighteen," I say.

"Hmmm." He nods approvingly. "You're quite the young commando here, aren't you? Taking charge and running the show."

"No, really I'm not. It's just, circumstances require."

"Circumstances *require*!" Da says, jumping up in the air a bit and clapping his hands loud as gunshots. It's like I have won some kind of talent show or something. "That's the thing, my boy, the thing, and the thing itself. When circumstances *require*, what are you capable of?"

He has the whole room staring.

"The man is proud of his grandson," Jarrod says to Matt.

"So he is, so he is. Wanna buy a Glock, kid?"

"Jeez, no," I say, physically recoiling.

"Right, another day," Matt says.

"Hey, if you can't locate the right stuff," Jarrod says, "maybe we can just find something off the shelves here to help him out."

"Jarrod," I snap. "That is my grandfather."

"I don't mind," Da says.

"Listen, gents, come back in a couple hours, I'll have you all sorted out," Matt says.

"Um," I say, taking charge a little less authoritatively than my new rep might suggest. I lean a bit closer. "About payment . . . we're a bit light right now, trying to avoid cash machines . . ."

He looks right past me. He looks hard and soft at Da as Da tries to coolly not look at the wares on offer everywhere we turn.

Matt shakes his head slightly. "I know that look. I know all about it. Call it a gift, from my uncle."

I am about to open my mouth to thank him, find it already hanging wide open, start to speak, but stop. Matt pulls out a small lunch bag tightly wrapped in tape, whips it punishingly hard into Jarrod's midsection. "Besides, this guy right here is three of my best customers."

We walk down the tired, gray main drag, killing time and being anonymous.

"Wanna bone up?" Jarrod says, because that's what Jarrod says, and he is walking around with a rock band's monthly supply.

"The answer is yes," Da says. Hunching over a bit, smoking on his cigarette as if he is trying to get things out that are just not in there.

"The answer is no," I say. I put my arm around Da, and he feels a lot less substantial than the guy who loosened my tooth. "Why don't we just get something to eat?"

"One small smoke, I swear," Jarrod says, "then eat. I'm buying, even."

This is an attractive offer. I took a few hundred dollars out of the ATM before we fled, but that wouldn't last long without a lot of help. I am about to say okay when Da pushes me over the edge.

"Please?" he says.

No matter what his stories. No matter what his tall tales, and I have no idea which ones are redwoods and which have some reality. No matter, no matter, I know the old guy did not go through his life as a chimney like Jarrod.

He just wants to feel better. Any kind of better. Before his mind started the tricks, he was frequently in this kind of stoop-over or that kind of organ discomfort. The blinking lights in his attic sometimes made the physical pains skitter into the shadows. But now, when the meds are not balanced just so, they all seem to come slithering out of the corners.

"Fine. A little. Jarrod, a little by standards other than yours."

"Promise," he says.

We wander around the gritty town that we don't know and

that doesn't appear to want to know us. But this being this kind of town, there has to be an overgrown baseball field around someplace for just this sort of thing.

It takes mere minutes for us to find it, and we are sitting on the bench along the third base line. Where there used to be four slats for baseball butts, there are two, but that is plenty for us. Jarrod does the assembly work, Da smokes another cigarette and stares out over the playing field and the smoke and the overgrowth and time, the way smoking always seems to allow an older person to do. Almost seems worth the smoking for, losing some years at the end of your life, in order to have all that screen time with your younger self.

"You ever play?" Da asks out loud.

"Sure," I say quickly. "You know—"

He slaps my thigh, hard. "I know you did," he says calmly. "I remember every pitch you threw, every one you hit, every one you missed. I will forget my feet before I'll forget any of that. I was asking him."

"Me? Ya, I did," says Jarrod.

"Very good," Da says, looking over the short chain-link fence curving around the outfield.

"Except, you didn't," I correct.

"Hey, if he can make up stuff, so can I?" Jarrod says, risking a broken nose or something.

No such thing. Da just sits, still staring. He takes on that creased, crunched expression folks get when they are asked a question they know they should know, they know they do know, only they don't know it right now. He looks frustrated and confused and reluctant, but he takes the joint when it is passed. Then he smokes and extends it to me, and I am so close to asking him if he indeed knows which of his stories is true and which is otherwise, I can actually feel that *W* forming on my lips.

"No, I can't," I say, and he withdraws.

Jarrod takes the smoke back. I start walking, and point at him as menacingly as I am able.

"I will be right back," I say. "Do not go anywhere. And do not lose him."

"How could I even do that? He's, like, full size."

I run up to the corner, where we passed one of those discount stores. Probably was a five-and-dime once, a Woolworth's, a dollar store, a whatever-the-name-says, but always cheap as cheap and always the kind of place you could get a Wiffle bat and ball but most likely not authentic Wiffle brand.

That's not exactly what I am looking for, anyway. I find what I want, a sponge ball, orange, and an enormous fat bat, plastic but three times the strength of and about twelve times the barrel width of a Wiffle bat.

I buy four of those balls. Because I am feeling very jacked right now and some balls are going to go downtown.

Next thing, I am standing at home plate. I look out at the fence. How did it get so close? How did the whole field get so small? I feel like I could touch the left field foul pole with the tip of the bat. I played Little League and Babe Ruth League and hit a fair few long balls before I stopped respecting baseball enough to work hard and compete with the guys who did.

Da hated that. Hated it so much, the notion of being good enough at something but not giving it the proper respect.

"Suck with dignity," he said at the one game of mine he ever booed me and walked off from, "but don't suck with apathy."

Even when I was good, though, the fence always seemed so far away, such a tall order, not within my reach. Now I'm embarrassed that I ever felt that way.

Suddenly there is Da, on the mound. He has one orange ball in his right hand, one in his left, and two at his feet.

"You," he says, long past the possibility of committing Jarrod's name to memory, "out there and shag flies."

"They are too small for me," Jarrod says, giggling from the bench.

"Get out there and play some outfield," Da shouts, and Jarrod jumps.

My cousin camps in center field, and Da waves him over to left. Farther. Farther.

"Come on," Jarrod whines, "I'm going to have to run a long way if he hits it over there."

"He won't. He can't. He was too lazy to learn to use the whole field. He could only pull and everyone knew it and that's why he sucked."

I laugh out loud. Jarrod laughs out loud. The pitcher himself turns in my direction and stares me down.

"Bring it, old man," I say.

For someone of his age and limitations, Da's windup and delivery are sweet, as they always were. He rears back, lifts the left knee up about ten inches, extends the left elbow straight at me, comes straight over the top with his right hand, and lets go of the ball at the optimal release point. Straight it comes.

It whistles in fast, and *pap*, smacks me right in the ear.

"Hey," I shout, pointing the fat red bat in his direction. "You did that deliberately."

"Of course I did. Get back in the box."

I get back in the box, ready to swing. He winds up, unloads one straight and meaty in the middle of the strike zone. I am so excited, by the moment and the ball and the fence, that I swing so hard I pull a chest muscle; I feel it instantly.

I make contact, though, and the ball leaves the infield.

Dribbling harmlessly along the ground, then slowed by the tall grass, right to where Jarrod is waiting for it. He doesn't even have to move.

The pitcher laughs. The left fielder laughs.

"Bring it, old man," I say, because it has been a long time since I taunted a pitcher, so I am short on material.

He brings it.

"Ow." I drop the bat. "Da, that really stings. If you do that again . . ."

He starts walking toward me, bouncing on the balls of his feet. I may have found the cure for old age here. "Yeah? You'll what?"

He backs me down. "Nothing. Just pitch."

"I will. But if you whine one more time, next thing I hit you with is a rock."

I dig in silently. He winds up with the third ball.

And smacks me in the ear again. If there was a game of ear hitting, he would be world senior champion. But we are not playing that game. We are playing a very different game.

I shut my face. He winds up with the fourth ball. He slings it.

He jams me on the hands and I hit another dribbler to Jarrod.

"Damn," I say, digging in once more. The old man is laughing, pleased at still topping me, pleased I am no longer moaning. He winds up and throws.

I cream the ball. I murder it, and it does not go to any stupid damn left field, either. I have mashed the ball high in the air and as straight to dead center as possible, and Jarrod is making a lame attempt to get out there, but that is pointless, people, because I have gotten *all* of that one.

I am running the bases, shocked at how thrilled I am over this. Over the fence. I hit one *out*. I look as I round first toward second, to see the ball land.

It's only about a foot beyond the fence. Jarrod is actually in position, and he reaches up, and if the ball hadn't bounced right off his forehead, he would have caught it. I hit that with everything I had.

I am elated and defeated, all in one go.

I still do my homerun trot because at least I can taunt Da, which I do, pointing a big finger his way and hooting at him as I hit third.

But he's not watching. He's not listening. He's not *here*.

Still looking up at some spot where the ball may or may not have crossed the sky several seconds ago, Da steps sideways off the mound, stands there looking up awkwardly, hands held out for balance. Then he looks at me, awkwardly, lost, and falls sideways, landing on his hip.

"Da," I say, running straight across the diamond. I get to him, pick him up, and he winces.

"Are you okay?" I ask. "I am so sorry, this was a stupid idea. I am sorry. Are you all right?"

He stares at me. He stares and stares and stares.

It is a sandwich shop, about ten booths and a ten-foot counter. Smells like coffee. Smells like tomato soup. Smells like just enough Lysol to be reassuring.

Soup and sandwich times three.

"He will be fine," I say to Jarrod, who looks uncharacteristically worried.

"He doesn't look good, Danny."

"He'll be fine, once he gets his stuff."

"That's what we all say."

"Food, for strength, then some medication, get his equilibrium back, then a good rest and he will be his old self."

"His old, old, old self, " Jarrod quips.

I reach right across the table and grab his shirt, pulling him to me to make the booth seem a lot smaller. A teenage girl pushes a stroller across in front of us and stares as if we can't see her. As if we are in a jackass aquarium or something. Don't tap the glass, girlie.

I look at my balled fist, Jarrod's balled shirt, the uncomfortable defenseless look on his face.

"How many times do you suppose this table has seen this scene?" I ask with what I hope is an apologetic smile.

Jarrod shrugs. "Probably, like, a lot?"

"What is even in this for you, man?" I ask him, still clinging to him.

"I don't know," he says.

I laugh. "You're a good man," I say right up close to his face.

"The bar on the opposite corner is that kind of place," says the cook with the Marty Van Buren sideburns. It sounds like a joke but he appears unamused. He delivers the soups and sandwiches himself, separating the goings-on by plunking down food. The waitress is having her own food at the counter.

He walks away. I look to Da beside me and he looks rather drained of color.

"Eat," I tell him, picking up half of his tuna sandwich, which is now bleeding watery mayo onto him. He takes the sandwich listlessly, dunks a corner into his tomato soup so that both sandwich and soup mingle into a look that could kill your appetite. He bites, crunches into too much celery.

I am very happy I got ham and cheese.

"What is your plan, Danny Boy?" Jarrod asks.

"My plan?" I ask. "What kind of plan could I have? I was going off to study *philosophy* in a few weeks, that was my plan. And even that was no kind of plan at all."

Jarrod nods.

"It has to be getting worse by the day, man," I say. "Worse for me and him both. There will be a lot to answer for, even criminal stuff, who knows. All I can say is, he's in trouble down there, and I am not bringing him back into that, no way. I can't."

Jarrod nods.

I look over to Da to see that he's getting along okay. Half the sandwich is gone, even the crust, and he is working at the soup. The management must have split a small bag of potato chips among the three of us because there are about five chips per plate and a slice of pickle, but nobody's eating all that anyway. Da smiles a bit, winces, smiles, dunks his sandwich. I take this as progress.

Jarrod has eaten everything. Now he's collecting pickles and chips that don't belong to him, but hey.

"I'll take him," Jarrod says.

"What?"

"I'll take him. He can live with me. At least for a while. He can share my boiler room, and as long as he does his quiet-old-guy thing more than his nutty-old-guy thing, we could probably get away with it."

Stress is about to cause me to blow, to grab him again and emphasize how stupid and reckless the plan is.

Until I picture it.

"What?" he says, smiling broadly but uncertainly. "What? What's so funny? Dan . . ."

I love this laugh. It feels so good it just perpetuates itself. Then Jarrod catches it; then, Da. It is joy.

The waitress comes over with our bill, hands it to the old guy, and says cheerfully, "Thank goodness for stoners, or we'd never move this food."

We walk back into Venus Exotics, leaving Da in the car. He is in no running mood, a sore hip and a lit cigarette keeping him reliably planted in the backseat.

True to his word, Matt hands over a bag with a few pill bottles inside, just like the pharmacist does.

"I even gave you a little note with instructions inside, just like the pharmacist does," he says with no small pride. "You take care of that ol' boy. Sorry to say, kid, but I know that look. Good things don't usually follow that look."

It stings.

"So then, Matty, why don't you give us one of your other products, that give an old boy a look that good things definitely do follow?"

I did not say that.

Matt quickly reaches out and bops Jarrod on the side of the head with something like a baseball bat that isn't one. "There, that'll give you a look." He's laughing; now he's serious.

"Here's to wash it down," he says and grabs me a large can of something called POW energy drink off a shelf.

"Thanks," I say warily. "But is this going to make him feel anything more than we want him to?"

"Only a little extra consciousness, I'm afraid."

I shake his very warm, strong hand. I wait till I am out the door before giving it a precautionary wipe on my shirt.

We tear away in the Subaru after a successful excursion, feeling a little like maybe we can do this.

"All the best people are rascals," Da says as he takes this pill and this pill and this pill with a swig of POW and we all cross our fingers.

E I G H T

Moods are elevated as we make the last turn into the college. Right stuff or not, the medication seems to be combining well enough in my grandfather to have produced a goodwill and camaraderie that fills the car up nicely. We are all pretty much tired of driving for now, though, and everybody's looking forward to doing some nothing.

But that doesn't look like it's going to happen.

Jarrod quick-pumps the brakes before we get into the parking lot itself.

"Damn," he says. "There shouldn't be anybody here."

"What?" Da and I say.

I go a little bit frantic, and my newfound control and strength go floating like so much smoke straight out the passenger window.

Da remains slouched way back in the car, out of sight, as we sit and ponder.

"I got nobody else visiting, I swear," Jarrod says. "And that isn't any car connected to the college I know of. Nobody has been on campus for weeks, nobody is scheduled for another two, they always let me know in advance anyway, and if this is a student, lost and confused, it's way early for that."

Da's voice has dropped an octave.

"You didn't use that phone, like I told you not to, did you, Young Man?"

I am absolutely certain he hears my Adam's apple go *ga-lulk* right now.

"No," I say, clipped. "You took it, anyway, remember? So, see—"

"Did you call anyone, Daniel?"

Oh no. There are no *lies of omission* with Da.

"Yes, but I used a landline—"

"Who did you call?"

"Lucy," I say, flattened. "I called her cell from a pay phone."

"Drive," he tells Jarrod.

The driver tears away with surprising speed, and focus.

"Go easy," Da says. "Stealth is more important than speed. Stealth is more important than everything. They can't catch you if they don't chase you, so don't make them chase you."

I sit, hands folded, in the shotgun seat, and I believe if my grandfather had a shotgun back there, I would not be in any seat at all. I remain silent for as long as—

"That kind of screwup can be lethal," Da says to me coldly. "It may be yet."

"I am sorry, Da. I am so sorry. I wasn't—"

He punches the back of my headrest. I think it is not violence. I think I am beginning to learn the difference between what is and isn't violence. I think that was just "shut up."

"Driver," Da says.

"Yes, sir."

"Have you got one of those godforsaken cell phones?"

"Doesn't everyone?"

There is a barely nonviolent silence.

"Could you please loan your phone to my foolish grandson? His is back at the college. As long as they already know we are with you, one quick call won't hurt. GPS can't help them much if we are already right around the corner from them."

I take the phone, turn to Da.

"Phone your sister, please. Get what you can."

I do what I am told, as I will continue to do for as long as I know him.

"Lucy?"

"Dan? Now whose phone are you using?"

I try to focus through a separate conversation here in the car.

"We will need a place to stay quiet for a while," Da says.

"I know a guy," Jarrod says. "But I kind of figure you're the kind of guy who would know a guy."

"I am the kind of guy who would know a guy, but all those kind of guys I know are the kind of guys we don't want to know now."

"Um, what?"

"Do you know a place?"

"I do."

"Very good. For the time being, though, drive the opposite way to there."

"Why?" he asks.

I punch him in the arm and he complies.

"This is Jarrod's phone," I say.

"Please, Dan, just come home, all right? They are not going to do anything to you. But Granddad has done stuff that you don't even know. They just want to protect him and everybody else and just get him secure . . ."

The phone is one of those annoying ones that sound like a little radio broadcasting to everyone in the vicinity.

"Secure!" Da nearly vomits the word. "They want to make me secure. Isn't that just kindness itself."

"I think he can hear you," I tell her. "And he's not wildly in favor of your plan."

"Too bad. You have to stop this before it gets all serious."

"Did you rat us out?" I ask as Da gives my headrest a hurry-up punch.

"Why would I even have to do that? They were in my room so soon they practically hung up the phone for me. Please, Dan."

"How are Mom and Dad?"

"Livid!" Lucy shouts.

"Perfect," Da says with contempt.

"Tell them I miss them too."

"You are going to screw up everything," she says. "College and everything."

Because Lucy is crying as she says that last bit, I think I feel something. Something small but sharp and electric zings through my chest.

My sister, my pal, cares whether I have a future, and I care that she cares.

What a chump. Pair of chumps, really.

"It'll be okay, Luce. I can't just—"

"He's dangerous!" she shouts.

A highway crosswind or something suddenly blows Jarrod's attention in our direction. "Hiya, Luce."

Da reaches forward and grabs the phone from me.

"I think this is good enough," he says.

He rolls down his window and, with Lucy's little voice screaming DanDanDanDanDan like a tiny passing train, he takes his pick of the endless parade of pickup trucks passing us in the next lane, draws back that hellacious, accurate old right arm, and fires away.

The phone zips on a line and clatters around the bed of an old Dodge. And takes its GPS signal with it.

"I repeat," Da says, "technology is for chumps."

"I found that phone in a couch," Jarrod says. "It was perfect."

"Um, Da?" I venture with trepidation.

"Yes, Young Man."

"Won't they trace Jarrod's car?"

He punches my headrest again. Not becoming my favorite mode of communication. I miss my phone.

"Glad you are catching on, my boy. I guess we are going to have to locate ourselves another car after Jarrod gets off the next exit to head us north."

"I don't think so," Jarrod says.

I stiffen.

"Excuse me?" Da says calmly.

"It's not my car, so it's not registered to me. A student left it at the end of spring semester. Left it for the summer to go help stabilize things during the election in Haiti."

"'Stabilize,'" Da says, laughing. "I love that old chestnut."

"Thanks," Jarrod says, like he's achieved something.

"Where would we be without ya, J?" I say.

"It doesn't even bear thinking about," he says, turning off and heading us north.

"This is your guy?" I say when we pull down the narrow lane.

"Yup," Jarrod says.

"This is the same guy as the other guy."

"He's about the only guy I know. There is one other, but he's not gonna want to know me anymore when he finds out I stole his car."

"But why are we here, man?"

The combination of activities has conspired to leave my grandfather snoring in the backseat. I am jealous but there is no resting for me at the moment.

Jarrod points to an array of windows in a row above Matt's shop. "He rents out rooms. Nobody will find you here. Then you can make a plan for what to do next. He's good at plans, actually. He'll help."

I look up at the windows. There are little lacy curtains in each one, and a plastic flower in a milk glass. You can see the dust from the street. I have not the slightest doubt that Matt does all his decorating out of that dollar store where I got the baseball stuff.

It hits me now. Like hunger, like cramps, like the full burst in your belly when you drink an icy Coke after having nothing in your stomach during a whole scorching summer day.

I love baseball.

"Let's go talk to him," I say.

"Back for more already?" Matt says, laughing. He is closing up shop, no assistant helping him. "You guys are voracious."

"Got any rooms free, Matt?" Jarrod says.

"A couple. What's up, something wrong with *The Shining*?"

"We just need to move on now," I say, cutting Jarrod off before he can be more helpful.

Matt looks back and forth from one of us to the other and back again with a sly, knowing lip curl. "I get a lot of that here. No problem. Where's my pal?"

"He's in the car."

"He okay with stairs?"

"Why wouldn't I be okay with stairs?" Da says, walking in, bleary but with us. He is limping noticeably.

"No reason, pal," Matt says, though he is probably counting about five reasons in his head.

We follow him through the front door, then he lets us all in the entrance next door. We tromp up the dark and curved stairway that is no struggle even for Da because the stairs are uncommonly short. It's almost like floating up to the next level.

"Most people here are singles, ha-ha," he tells us quite unnecessarily, "but I do have one double room. You want three singles?"

"We'll take a double," I say quickly, not wanting even a hint of another ramble by Da to happen. I shudder at the thought of his taking off here like he did in the relative safety of the woodsy campus.

"One double, one single, then."

"Oh, just the double," Jarrod says. "I'm gonna drive back to my place."

Da snaps right to attention. I gasp. "Jarrod, oh, no, you can't."

"Right," Da says, "you can't."

"I have to be there," Jarrod says. "I have to. There are things to do. Those guys will sure be gone when I get there, then we can just go back like it all never—"

"No-no," Da says with finality. "Oh no, no, no. That cannot happen. You are a good boy, and have been wonderful to us, but you are going to have to be wonderful to us for at least a little while more."

Jarrod, in his endearing way, takes this as an invitation. As appreciation.

"Oh, really, nice and all, but thanks. I honestly do need to, you know, physically be back there at night. It's my job and everything so it's the least—"

"Really, no," Da says. In his special-serious voice.

"Jeez, even I got a chill off that one," Matt says with a laugh. "The elder statesman can get quite the snarl on when he wants to, huh?"

Jarrod sees less of the humor. He looks like he wants to cry.

"Easy, Da," I say, putting a hand on his hand.

He turns on me, eyes reddish. He pushes me away and approaches Jarrod to make his point a little clearer. Jarrod might just piss himself, and if the place didn't already smell like this when we got here, I might have guessed he'd already commenced.

Before Da can snort in his face, I grab him.

Really hard, really meaning it, I grab my grandfather's arm and yank him forcefully in my direction.

He is shocked as his piercing eyes rush up to mine.

"Oh no," he says to me. "Oh, no, no, no." He turns away again.

I yank him even harder. "Oh no yourself, Da. No, and no, and no. You leave him alone now."

He bites his lower lip and wrinkles his nose in a most threatening snarly dog fashion.

I stare, scared witless, but keeping that to myself.

He holds ground.

I hold ground.

Then I make my move.

I bring both hands up to my face, filling almost all the space between us.

"Shush," I say calmly, all eight fingers waving in the water between us. "Octo-shush."

I walk past him, frozen there, because waiting for his response would be weak. Showing I cared what he thought now would be weak.

Jeez, I wonder what he's thinking.

"Listen, Jarrod," I say, "you have to understand how it complicates things to have you go back. We will work something out, don't worry."

Two heavy hands thump on my shoulder, and I see Jarrod's eyes go B-movie horror wide.

"That's my boy," Da says in my ear. He kisses my cheek. "We're knocking that ridiculous fear thing right out of you. Now once we throttle that foolish compassion malarkey, you'll be the complete package. And I can go in peace."

It feels like what international peace talks must feel like, or trade negotiations, or big business deals. Jarrod, Matt, Da, and I sit around the folding card table that is the centerpiece of my room. The place is not bad at all, if you thought to consider what one of these dodgy hideaways might be like. There is a picture of Mount Kilimanjaro on one wall, the pyramids of Egypt on the opposite one. They look like they came free with the Sunday paper, but they are framed, from the dollar shop, making the investment modest but thoughtful. The window opposite the dark, planky gumwood door has the dusty plastic rose I saw from the street. There is a lot of little-engine-that-could about that rose and the spirit of the place.

There is no clock and no calendar, and no wonder. Please check all weapons and any sense of time passing at the front desk, to be collected on checkout.

There is so much smoke in the air, it has replaced my need for solid food for a couple of days. Matt's on cigar while the other two are at the Camels.

"So, you are going to study philosophy," Matt says.

"I am," I say, sideways, waiting for the punch line. There is always a punch line to philosophy.

"I studied philosophy," Matt says both proudly and whimsically.

I try to guess if that was actually the punch line and not actually true. I decide it is the punch line either way.

"Boston University. Time of my life. I was headed for magna cum laude, too. Till I got arrested and thrown out for training my ferret, Colin, to contaminate selected biomed labs. Damn, those were fun times."

Da exhales.

"So you were a terrorist?"

Uh-oh.

"Da . . . ?"

Matt waves me down. It's cool.

"Sir, you flatter me," Matt says. "I was a prankster. I was a rapscallion." He waves his cigar in a theatrical way. "But I was pretty good at it. And Colin was excellent. He was really the brains of the operation."

"It is all diversion," Da says. "Terrorism. Nobody knows what's really happening. Everything you see? In the news? That's what they want you to see. Killing and blowing up stuff? Who cares? We don't care. We *wanted* you to think the great threats were coming down out of the sky or rumbling right at you in a truck. Who cares? People die, a hundred, a thousand. Means absolutely nothing. Chumps, you are all chumps. Know what we have done? We have taken all you little babies, we have turned on the TV, turned it on loud and made it all fast and splashy and crashy, and plopped you damn babies on the floor to just sit there stupid and watch it, all day long. Idiots. Babies. You keep falling for it, so they keep broadcasting it. Watch the show, babies, watch the show."

Matt looks altogether impressed.

"I love this guy," Matt says. "I really do."

"He's very lovable," Jarrod says, hiding his skinny self behind his cigarette.

For his part, Da is showing a rapidly decelerating interest in being lovable.

"You were a terrorist?" he challenges Matt.

"Ah, actually you are the one who said that . . ."

No matter. "You don't even know who a terrorist is or what the terror is about. You all like explosions and blood and noise. It all works because you are all *morons*. Morons blow up other morons for the fear and amusement of yet other

morons, while the adults go about the real business of order-
ing and reordering the world."

"Reordering," Matt says, and he is saying his bit about as
pleasantly as you could say this stuff. "You mean killing as
many people as possible who do not agree with your ideology."

"Ha," Da says, as if Matt has dropped right into his carefully
constructed tiger trap. "Just shows you. You don't get the new
world at all. With the diabolical twenty-four-hour news cycles
and all that hounding us all the time, might as well make it work
for you. Only a dope kills 'em all. Killing, my friend, is yesterday's news. Killing is old-fashioned. Maiming is where it's at."

Matt is on the brink of being defeated, but clinging on.

"But, man, how could you do all that, for your own pur-
poses, when hundreds, thousands, of folks, people just like
yourself, suffer horribly for it?"

Da has been pushed back on his heels now. He looks back
and forth between me and Matt, bypassing Jarrod entirely.
He smiles suspiciously.

"Is this some kind of famous philosophy quiz-type thing?"
he asks.

"Ah, well, Da, it just sounds like a question to me."

"It is," Matt says. "It's just a question."

"Oh." Da nods, happy, friendly, like a guy who's just been
given the directions to the party and is damn grateful for
them. "In that case, the answer is: Why would I give a rat's
eyelash about a hundred, or a thousand, of *me*?"

There is a smoky silence descending that threatens to spoil
all this great fun, until Jarrod decides it is actually a trick
question, "I know this one, the answer is: You are your own
brother. Right?"

Da stares him melted. "You know what I did to my brother when the filth—"

"Da," I say, "come on, you're being a drag. Smoke a bone with Jarrod and tell one of your *funny* stories, like about the country you overthrew using nothing but fire ants."

He whips a look at me, as if *now* we have gone into dangerous reality. Then he turns back to Matt for the payoff.

"Okay, you want to know where your real terrorism is?"

"Ah, well, sure, that would be good to know."

I have never seen Da more serious. I have never seen anyone more serious.

"It's in your food," he stage-whispers. "I know, because I put it there."

Jarrod responds to all this levity by frantically breaking out his accessories for mood enhancement. His hands shake, but he is making a heroic job of getting something smokable assembled.

Matt looks, seriously, at Da, at me. He is undoubtedly a man who has seen, if not everything, certainly a telling cross section of everything. He could be harder than he is, I think. And he could be more cynical, for sure.

But he listens. He nods. He goes on about his business.

"You are one hot potato, sir," Matt says, shaking Da's hand.

Da takes it in the spirit offered, shakes it. "It's not the potatoes," he says, like offering a great and true tip to a select friend at the racetrack. "But beyond next year you'll want to be careful of pretty much everything else. And, oh, do buy American."

"You sound like my doctor now," Matt says, patting a modest belly. "Except for that little American thing at the end there."

"*Source carefully*, is what I'm telling you. Watch your eat and drink. You'll never see it coming. And it's already too late to try, 'cause it's in the chain."

Well, then. Where does a party or a business meeting or whatever go from there? Snacks?

"We don't have any clothes with us or anything," Jarrod says. "What are we supposed to do? What if I just went there, maybe grabbed a few things, hurried right back . . ."

"That site is toxic," Da says. "Can't go back. It's dead. Forget about it."

"Ever?" Jarrod asks.

"We'll see," Da says casually, like running everyone else's world is just second nature.

"He will need his life back at some point, Da," I point out.

"We'll see," he repeats, and I accept, silently reassuring Jarrod with an old-style, single-finger shush gesture.

I secretly upped Da's dose, and between one thing and another he is sleeping so soundly the snoring is volcanic music. Sitting at my chair, I stare out the open window, listening to him and the outside world clash. It doesn't go long without a horn beeping here, even in the night. It is usually joined by a responding beep, then things go quiet for a while more again. I listen to people talking as they walk to and from the pub, the movies, the restaurant, the park. Twos and fours are it, and a chunk of me now is wishing to be among them. I am looking forward to going to school. Going to a whole different world, away from my town and my family . . . and this new craziness, which has been unusual and exciting but is fast approaching do-without-it time. I don't have a great many friends back home, truth be told, so I don't know how much I'll be back once I make the leap. My folks sent me to a weird boarding school as a weekly boarder, the most unwieldy of all the configurations, I think. You don't live there full-time, so just when things get social and fizzy, you are going home for the weekend or holidays. Then you get to what's supposed to be home, and you are trying to hang with the folks who have been living the real part of life, five days out of the seven, without you. You are trying to hang.

Until you are not trying. Which was okay. I'm not complaining. Not a lot, anyway. At least I don't think it's a lot.

And the only one who ever came and visited me, was him.

I stand from the window and walk to his bedside. I stare down at the snoring stillness of him, and I shake my head.

The only one. This Chock Full o'Nuts I see before me.

Couldn't even plan for it, either, because he would just appear. Take me to dinner usually, or just drive around. He taught me how to drive so early, I had to relearn when it was time to go for my license. Had to take a handful of professional lessons because of all the bad little habits I developed, you know, like casually experienced drivers do.

Despite his own hall-of-fame smoking credentials, the one time he caught me trying it—one of his surprise appearances at my dorm window, of course—he took me outside and gave me bubbling and searing cigarette burns in the center of each palm. Looked just like stigmata for two weeks. Kids called me Jesus Smoking Christ all that time.

I liked it. The attention. All of it.

And it was almost like I didn't even have him, because

pretty much nobody ever believed me that he had been there. The only one who at least sometimes believed was Lucy.

"I believe you. He's psychotic," she said when I showed off my stigmata.

I sit on the side of the bed now, the snoring very comforting to me. Certain things, I realize lately, calm and settle me. Snoring means sleeping, good. Electric cars are a problem for me because they are so silent. That could kill you, right? Because a car is supposed to make noise to warn you of its lethality. That kind of incongruence in the physical world has begun to put me right off. Silence is deadly. Sound is life.

"Stealth, is all," Da says and I leap off the bed as if it were a catapult.

I stand with my back to the window, staring at him, staring, staring at him. But he has not changed. The slow up and down of his rib cage, the three coarse breaths, and then the chopping snore.

Did he even say it? Is he testing me further, playing with my mind? Can he hear inside my head, the old mystical-madness thing that attaches to altered minds?

I sort of wish I could have done my first year of philosophy before this small adventure. Next summer would have been a lot more convenient. Then maybe at least I'd have known a thing or two.

"Hey," comes a hoarse whisper, wafting up to my window from the street.

I turn to find Jarrod down there, alone.

"Come on down," he says.

"Get to bed," I say.

"Why?" he says.

I go to give him an answer, realize I haven't really got one, and head down into the night.

"I have an idea," he says as we sit on the curb watching absolutely nothing go by.

"Don't. Don't do that, Jarrod. Don't have an idea."

"Hear it, hear it. The old man is dead to the world, right?"

"Hmm. Not quite yet but, anyway . . ."

"We make a rapid run. Back—"

"Stop it, will you? No."

"Listen. We are back in an hour and a half, collect our stuff all up, nobody's the wiser. Perfect plan. If you come with me, you don't have to worry that I'll screw everything up. We'll have Matt bolt the door from the outside—he has to do that sometimes—so even if he wakes up, your Da is safe and sound."

When he finally stops talking, I breathe in the refreshing silence.

Then, "Leave it, Jarrod. My stuff is gone. Your stuff is gone."

"Why would they take my stuff? My stuff is still there. Probably yours, too. You can get the rest of Da's things, the clothes. You can get the phone and everything. It's perfect. It's perfect."

The desperation is as clear as the greasy sweat on Jarrod's face.

"It's all gone, Jarrod. All of it. Forget it. They took everything, for sure."

"Not everything. I'm a good hider. A good hider."

He is speaking both faster and slower than usual. The words themselves burst out quick, with wrong-long air spaces between them. It's like a verbal version of the game we played as kids, 1-2-3-red-light.

"What is it, Jarrod?"

"What is what? I want to go home, remember? That's it. I just told you."

"What is it you have to go back for, that can't wait?"

"My stuff. And it's where I live now. And I got work in the morning. You know how you just don't feel right when you're not in your place?"

"I am getting to know that feeling pretty well, yeah."

"Right. Then. Let's go."

He is actually leaning his upper body in the direction of his car.

"Will I guess what it is?"

He stops leaning and looks at the ground. "No, why don't you not do that."

"You already have a load of stuff from Matt, so I know it isn't that. So it's . . . other stuff?"

"Stop it, huh, Danny, please? Can't you just leave me be? I feel worse enough already."

"Ah cripes, Jarrod. You know, it's these kinds of reasons why you are what is known as a ne'er-do-well."

"Are you trying to insult me? With ne'er-do-well? Cousin, I'd ne'er do any-damn thing at all if I could get away with it."

This is very much like punching water.

"So . . . dammit . . . just get something from Matt."

"Not possible," he says, putting two hands up in front of him, as if I was coming to kick his ass. Which I should do. "Not possible there, man, so let's just forget I said anything. Okay. Just let that one go."

"I think that's a good idea. Because I can assure you,

whatever you left behind is with somebody else now. And you don't want to go inquiring about it."

An old, old scratchy voice comes down at me from over my shoulder.

I look up and back, to my window.

"Jeez, Old Boy, who are you, Rasputin? What does it take to pin you down, even for one night?"

"Who is that?" He is pointing at Jarrod, and he isn't pleased.

"Just sharing a smoke. I'll be right up."

"You'd better be. I don't like the look of him."

He pulls his head back inside.

"I don't like the look of me, either," Jarrod says, dejected.

"See, it never would have worked anyway. Do this: Light up, smoke your brains out, and crash. Sleep in here in the capital of nowhere, in the state of oblivion, wake up all new, and we'll figure out a move. Okay?" I give him a heavy and honest hug around the shoulders.

He doesn't answer with words, but he does spark up a sapling. He inhales joylessly.

"That's the spirit," I say, and head upstairs.

NINE

People don't want to suck, said Da. They just do.
  I will never lie to you, he said. Unless I feel like I need to.
  People need witnesses, to behave.
  People need to be unobserved, to be themselves.
  They said they had a treatment for his condition. They said.
  The silent treatment, I said.

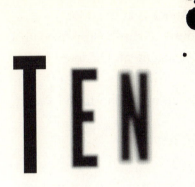

TEN

I am finding that I can sleep anywhere, and sleep fairly well. I didn't not know this before, but I didn't know it either. I just didn't notice.

With all the business lately, I have noticed. I sense this will be a welcome attribute over time.

Early morning, wherever we are, sounds like early morning elsewhere with the window open. The soothing sound of light traffic in the distance, the clank of a delivery truck dropping crates of bottles on the sidewalk. Urban seagulls menacing everybody. It's a comfort.

I roll over to find Da on his side, curled up in my direction, snuffling like a proper little old man and needing a shave. The pyramids float above his back, and a breeze sends the curtains to try and get a tickle at his patchy head. His hairline is at just about half tide. I notice he is balding asymmetrically, as well.

As well.

The door is at our feet, and a knock is at the door.

I sit up. "Matt?" I say cautiously. I hardly suspected this would be a bed-and-breakfast arrangement. Da doesn't stir.

"It's not Matt," the voice says.

"My god, Lucy," I say, jumping up in my shorts and T-shirt, rushing to the door.

I am about to stupidly open it.

"Who's with you?"

"Nobody. I swear on Grandma's grave." She was always a Grandma gal, so this is bankable.

I open the door, yank her inside.

"Ouch," she says.

"Ouch yourself. What is going on? What are you doing here? How did you *find* us?"

She stares me up and down for a second, then beyond me toward Da.

"How are you? Are you all right?"

"Lucy!"

"Okay, Jarrod brought me, but don't kill him."

"I'll kill him."

I go for the door, but she grabs my arm.

"Fine, but kill him afterward. He didn't mean any harm."

"He never does. Junkie jackass."

"He was just there, showed up really late . . . and I was waiting. I was hoping you would come back. That you would have the sense . . ."

"You were planted there. Is that what you mean?"

"No. That's not—"

Another knock. I rush to open it.

Jarrod puts up both hands in that "don't beat me up" sign.

I drive straight through that sign.

I burst through the doorway, grab him with both hands, drive him into the opposite wall. Then I begin slapping him sloppy. Backhand and forehand, across the mouth, bringing out blood from both sides and spraying it around the wall behind him.

I have so many things to say to him, to ask him, like why the hell did you do this, like what were you thinking, like are you a total mental defective or are you criminally sadistic, but I cannot think of one of those questions or any of its answers that are not going to flip the switch that will turn this beating into something more like *violence*, until I simply make the carefully reasoned decision to just keep on. So I hit him, belt him, slap, smack—don't close the fist, Dan, don't close the fist—until he is just too heavy for me to hold up anymore with Lucy on my back, pounding and even biting at my ear, so I drop him against the baseboard.

Where he slumps, sobbing and bleeding, the hot coffees drooling out of the bag in his left hand, and some manner of fresh-baked goods hotly greasing their way out of the other.

He brought us breakfast.

My whole body is shaking with this.

Look at him.

Dan. Danny. Look at him.

I step back and slam the door shut. Never happened.

"What has happened to you?" Lucy says, opening the door. Jarrod is scrabbling to his feet, the breakfast left as a dying, oozing thing on the floor. He gives up on standing and joins it there, sliding right down the wall with his back.

"Criminal stupidity," I say in Jarrod's direction. "Just add it to the list. Because thanks to you, they will be here any minute with a long list of all our crimes and misdemeanors, and a very short list of our futures. For those of us who had them."

Jarrod leans on the wall for support, tries to hold his blood in with his hand over his mouth, holds his balance with his other hand flat on the floor. Tries to talk to me. "It's okay, Danny Boy. It's okay, 'cause I told Lucy to turn off her phone."

This. This is what Da is trying to warn me about. Be cool, keep your wits about you. Decide what needs to be done and be prepared to do it. Your head rules. Your head is the almighty, your heart is the devil, deceptor.

Stupidity is a crime, punishable and unacceptable, no matter how nice a guy is.

"Lucy?"

She will not trifle with me here, this much I know.

"Did you turn your phone off?"

"No, Dan. In fact, I was talking on it mostly the whole time I followed behind Jarrod's car."

I stare flames at Jarrod in front of me, listen to my sister as she walks around behind me to check the death-sleep of the old man. I know his breathing like nobody does. I know he's fine.

"They did send me for you, Dan," she says. "Nobody is coming after you yet, because they sent me. It's me, right? Lucy. Don't be all paranoid. I'm giving you a chance. To just bring him back. Let it go. He has done wicked things, Dan. More than you even know, I'm sure."

"Sure? Being sure is for chumps, Lucy."

"Fine, whatever. But he is dangerous."

"You know who he's a danger to? Only to the guys who are just like him. Or just like he used to be. He's harmless, Luce."

"He is dangerous. Seems like he's making you dangerous, too."

"We are not dangerous. We are misinterpreted."

"Fine, whatever."

"Please stop saying that," I say through gritted teeth.

"Right. The thing is, they have a procedure now that can help him. Because of who he is, he's lucky. He has friends, he has access. He needs this, and I think you should make it possible."

She is making me angry. I breathe slowly and think, head over heart.

The stillness is torn by Jarrod's unexpected contribution.

"Makes a lot of sense to me," he says, all mush-mouthed.

And it's like somebody way off, much farther up the pipeline, has just turned a valve and let off about 50 percent of the pressure. I feel the powerful urge to laugh.

It makes a lot of sense.

To Jarrod.

It makes *sense*, to *Jarrod*.

I walk up to him, the mess at the base of the wall outside the little room above the porn shop. He cowers like I am there to stomp him into a form of lifelessness different from the one he already inhabits.

"No," I say, laughing a little, reassuring him. If there is such a thing as a lovable toxic sight, this is it. I reach out and playfully grab each of his ears. I toggle his head around, and around, and he smiles, all blood and innocence.

You'd have to be a beast, I think, looking at the blood.

"Please, Dan," he says, and I notice he stops smiling, tears are in his eyes. "Please? I won't . . . you're hurting me. Dan-o, it's me . . ."

I am squeezing his ears now. Twisting them, pulling them, tearing a little.

Jarrod puts his hands up, but does nothing to stop me hurting him. He lays his hands lightly on top of mine, and I feel it.

"Jesus," I say, taking my hands off his ears, placing them alongside his cheeks.

He stays frozen there, covering his ears. "Sorry, Dan-o," he says. "Sorry."

I nod at him. What I want to do now is to hug him. Instead, I just hold his cheeks, just like that. "I am protecting my grandfather," I say, pathetically. It feels true. It feels stupid. I am worthless. I can't protect anybody.

I feel his jaw muscles flex beneath my fingers as he speaks, "Do you think your grandfather might be protected by your pulling my ears off?"

That answer should be easy.

"I don't know," I answer.

He nods. "Okay, but if you do, go ahead."

Lucy is tapping my shoulder. I look up.

"Do you set bunnies on fire these days too, big man?"

She tugs me up away from Jarrod and walks over to where Da lies.

"Hiya, Granddad," Lucy says, as the Old Boy stirs.

She has sat on the side of his bed and is brushing a sad strand of his yellowed gray hair aside. I have turned in time to see his dawning, blinking, squinting entry into this weird and wondrous world that has bloomed in his absence.

Then I see his eyes go wide with terror and shock, followed by his hand shooting out like a bolt.

He is choking Lucy with such strength they are both instantly blue with the strain.

"Da," I say, jumping down and prying at his fingers. His has a grip like an eagle's talon.

"Ella," he rasps. His wife. Our grandmother.

Lucy gags, tries screaming.

I have to punch him. I do, twice, in the cheek.

She jumps up, clutching at her own throat. He rolls over and cowers, panting, as if she was the one who attacked him.

"It's the condition, Lucy," I say. "Are you okay? Did he hurt you? He didn't mean to hurt you. He hasn't had his meds yet."

She is whistle-breathing, but certainly it is at least partly an act.

"We are not going with you, Lucy."

She wheezes.

"You could help us out, though. Just forget you found us. Give us a chance. He deserves a chance. I have to save him."

She chokes again. Very dramatically.

"Start running, brother," she says. "I couldn't care less if you saved him now. I was never really even into him before, frankly. Now . . . to hell with him."

She walks to the door, where she walks just about into Matt.

"Well," he says approvingly, "*now* we're getting somewhere. Is this a party?"

She shoves past him, steps over Jarrod. Da squeals something unintelligible behind me, and I feel that urge to laugh again.

That urge goes away very quickly.

"Danny!" Lucy shrieks from the hallway.

I rush out to find her path blocked by one of the other nightcrawlers Matt has rented a room to. He is almost as burly as the landlord, but a whole lot more oily. He is standing spread across the whole narrow hallway. He has a hand down his sweatpants and the other one is pawing the air in Lucy's direction.

I run down the hall, practically knocking my sister down on the way to the guy. I crash right into him, and he is soft. He doesn't move much, but he is backed off.

"Jeez, pal," he says, like he is unaware of anything unright on his part. Like he is a victim of something.

"Did he touch you?" I ask my sister.

"Only . . . just, nothing much, no matter."

"Just get out of here, right?" I say, pointing to his open door and making a stupid little fist with my other hand.

"Whatever, whatever," he says, still working his pants hand. As he backs away he looks at Lucy with a leer and the most stomach-churning fat-lizard tongue flick imaginable.

Lucy actually makes a retching sound.

"Just get in there, creep," I say, so tough.

"That's it?" Da says from just outside our door.

I am surprised to find him there when I turn. "What?" I say.

"That's your *sister*," Da says with naked disgust for me.

"I recognize her, thanks."

"It's fine now," Lucy says. "Leave it."

"That is your sister."

"What am I supposed to do?"

"You can't figure that out? You get all worked up to smack

the crap out of your defenseless little junkie friend, and suddenly you run fresh out of outrage, is that it?"

"All right, leave it, will you? I feel bad enough over—"

"You know what you are supposed to do."

"No, I don't, Da. Leave it alone. I did enough."

"Yes, you do know. What, is little Lucy supposed to defend herself? Or maybe you just want to come back over this way, punch Jarrod around a little more, make yourself feel better, that'll show 'em, huh?"

"Stop it, Da," Lucy says.

He speaks, low and direct, like straight into my skull, like she's not even there anymore. "You know, Young Man."

"Really? I do? Do I?"

"No!" Lucy shouts.

Jarrod makes a low oh-no sound and disappears into the room. Matt starts making his way toward us, smiling. Da is right behind him.

"Shut the hell up out there, I'm trying to concentrate," the greasy man calls. I look into the room and he is lying on top of the bed, still looking out our way. And he is *working* it.

Even his bedspread looks made of bacon fat.

"Oh, no, you are not," I say and stomp into his room.

The man gets to his feet, but I meet him with two hands clamped hard on his throat. I squeeze his neck and drive him backward, bouncing his head crisp off the wall.

"No," Lucy shouts, sounding angrier. At me? How's that work?

"This what you mean, Da?" I say as I choke the guy purple.

"It's a start," Da says. "Nobody messes with your nearest and dearest. That cannot happen."

"Am I a good boy, then?"

"Eh, pretty good," he says.

"All right, all right," the guy rasps.

"Funny with those hands, are you, pal? Hey, Matt," I call. "Have a seat here for a second, wouldja?"

Matt comes over and has a bulky sit-down on the man's chest. All the wind oofs out of the guy, but he seems happy enough to be breathing. His arm dangles out to the side, and I grab it.

"This is your business hand, is that right?"

"Yes, I noticed that too," Da says.

"Do I know what to do, Old Boy?"

"I think you do, Young Man."

I think I do, too. I seize that disgusting paw, and I slam it flat on the squat night table. I pick up the marble cube of a night lamp, like a big, sharp-edge paperweight with a shade, and I slam it down on the hand. I slam it down on the hand. The man screams with horror as once more I slam the lamp down on his pervy, hairy hand.

With the third slam I feel the seam crack in the marble. With the forth, the seam splits completely and the man stops screaming and starts whimpering.

That's what we wanted. You don't always know beforehand when you want something, but you know when you get it.

As bad as I felt after smacking Jarrod around, before and after smacking Jarrod around, that is how good I feel now.

What the hell happened?

I don't remember when I felt better about myself.

As I walk out of the room I hear Matt behind me telling the guy, "You're going to have to pay for that lamp, Sammy."

"Where is Lucy?" I ask Da.

He shrugs. "I think she left in the commotion."

"Luce?" I call.

"Feel the difference?" he says, almost warmly.

I go running after her.

"It had to be done," Da says as I run. "It had to be done, and you done it, Young Man."

I catch up with her a hundred yards up the street, almost to her car. I put my arm around her shoulders and walk with her.

"So, have you enjoyed your big day out up here? Be planning another holiday here sometime soon? I never noticed before, but you're kind of a trouble magnet, you know that?"

She shoves my arm away and practically out of its socket. "This place is a bucket of pus," she snaps. "You guys should buy a house here, settle down, run for city council."

"Hey," I protest, "I was just up there defending your virtue."

"My *virtue* does not need you. And anyway, I don't know what you were doing, but you weren't doing that, that's for sure. Being your grandfather's perverse, violent sock puppet, that's what it looked like to me."

She presses the button on her key ring and her car beep-beeps at us.

"You don't understand," I say. "It is so much more than that. It is so much more."

She acts as if I am not even talking. She gets into the car, starts it up, revs the engine a lot more than necessary. She rolls down the window.

"I do hope you come back from this trip, Danny. I'd really love to see you again."

"What's that supposed to mean?"

She sighs. "Don't get in front of my car. Violence runs in families, you know. And I'm in the mood."

I laugh. I jump out as she pulls from the curb.

She guns it, clips me at the hip, spinning me around and leaving me bouncing on the pavement.

ELEVEN

"Valhalla."

That is Da's answer when I ask him where he wants to go. If he has any thoughts about where to go next, because time is the thing we have the least of, of all the things we have very little of.

Like money, strength, friends, or family support. Very little of all that, but even less of time.

"Valhalla, Da? Isn't that in New York state?"

He smiles, like I have said something profoundly stupid.

Matt has come and gone, again. Wished us all the best, again. Said to come back, again, anytime. He wasn't bothered by the acts of not-so-random violence going on in his tidy little cells, as there is no one on this earth with the flaps to challenge his power of unflappability.

He did, however, take just about all of my money.

"All of it?" I asked as he counted my meager stash. "Can I maybe write you a check?" I asked.

"Can I write you this?" he asked, pulling out of his pocket one of those leather covered lead deals for industrial-strength head-cracking.

"Maybe you should just post a 'no checks accepted' sign?"

"Nothing says 'I mean it' like a blackjack, though."

Even saying that, he sounded friendly.

"I'm going to have to get one of those," I said.

"I'm your man," he said. "Once you have money, of course."

So Da and I hit the street with *nothing*. Less than nothing, even. We are standing in this place in the clothes we wore yesterday, the only clothes we have. No phones, one wallet, mine, which serves no purpose now other than to add four ounces of artificial flesh to my bony self. A few days of medication, which is already showing signs of doing the patient little good. And the certainty that failure of a more severe kind is speeding up the highway toward us as we speak.

I get a nudge. I turn.

"Ugh, jeez, Jarrod, wash your face, at least."

He is standing there on the sidewalk looking like a scarecrow made from strips of veal, 8-ball eyes, and lips torn off a blobfish.

"Here," he says, holding out his car keys.

"What?"

"I screwed you up. I ruined everything. You were doing fine. You were going to win, and I blew it. Now look at you, you both look like crap, you're out on the street and the end is near."

"Hey, Mr. Sunshine," I say, smiling at him.

Somehow, incredibly, he manages to return a smile to me. It tears his lip right open and the blood flows, making him now a meat-faced scarecrow with a vivid red chin cleft.

"I thought we killed him already," Da says.

"Na," I say. "It was on our to-do list, but we've been busy."

"Come on, take it," Jarrod says, jangling the keys at me. "I just filled it yesterday. Subarus are brilliant on mileage, so you can go real far on what you have."

"Subarus suck," Da says. "Never catch me in one of them."

I laugh.

"Thing is, Jarrod, man, they know the car now. You showed Lucy, remember?"

"I wish we had more time with Lucy. I hadn't seen her in ages."

I do not understand Jarrod at all. It's not the drug use and the cracks-of-society nature of his relationship to civilization or any of that. That stuff you can work out, in a clinical enough way.

I don't understand the relentlessness of his heart.

"Listen, Jarrod, I am really, really sorry. For what I did up there. I am shocked, myself, that I reacted like that. I swear to you I never do that."

He pinches his lip together like a clamp before he smiles. "For somebody who never does that, you're kind of good at it."

I laugh, but I blush at the same time. I am ashamed.

"Ha," Da says, looking sharp, lucid, and sly.

"Ha, what?" I say.

"Ha," he says, pointing at me.

I am driving. Da insisted on front seat, Jarrod is fine with the back. North is where I am headed, because it just seems to me that from here, north is where all the nothing is.

"It's kind of pointless at this point, I'm afraid," I say.

"What?" Jarrod says.

"Driving anywhere. I mean, I don't know where to go, they are bound to catch us within hours, and even if this were a muscle car, we'd never be able to get away from anybody who really wanted to catch us."

"Nobody wants to catch you two, so don't flatter yourselves," Da says. The in/out nature of his condition is far more like streetlights than ever before. He is with us and gone again just that quickly. "You've never done anything."

It is a statement both reassuring and cutting.

Not to mention inaccurate.

"I may have done a few things," Jarrod says modestly.

I sigh. "Do I want to know these things, Jarrod?"

"You might not."

"Okay, then. Anyway, Da, we all agree you are the grand prize. But I am not looking forward to facing people at this point either. I just need . . . a little time and space to work out just what is the right thing."

"Ha," Da says.

"Ha, again?"

"'Right thing.' Phrase always makes me go ha."

"I might know a place," Jarrod says.

"I thought you were out of places?" I say.

"No, I said I was out of guys. But I know a place where you go to find a guy, who might know a guy . . ."

"At this point, men, that sounds like our kind of place," I say.

Because they know our vehicle, we are traveling rural roads all the way. The place Jarrod described would have taken another three or four hours if we took the main highway, but the way we have to snake through the region will take at least two times that, possibly three. The radio crackles in and out, usually coming up with one form of hillbilly music or heavy metal, and if you didn't know better you'd think we were one very alternative family off for a little backwoods vacation with the happy-clappy youngster in the back singing along to the tunes with his own made-up lyrics all the way. Suddenly he pipes up, "Oh, and did I tell you, Dan-o, you were wrong. When I went back to the college, those guys had *not* found the secret hiding place for my stash. Cool, or what?"

So, as it sinks in that I am tooling the byways at the helm of what is now almost certainly an officially reported stolen car, transporting a fugitive secret-spilling spook of an old man, we cheerfully add to the gumbo the fact that we are carrying consignments from two distinctly different classes of controlled substances. Three if you count the prescription medications that we purchased with no prescriptions. And they probably will count that, so, three.

"Congratulations, Jarrod." What else is there to say, really?

My Da cannot read my mind, though sometimes it does appear that way. He can, however, still read signs of a situation as well as anyone anywhere.

"You have to lose him, you know," he says icily.

"What?" I look at him, the road, him again.

"Watch the road."

"No. I mean I got the road. We're not losing him."

If talking about Jarrod in highly worrying terms registers

with him at all, he is not highly worried about it. He is even singing "Jolene" along with Dolly Parton, though he appears to believe it's "Moline."

"Lose him, Young Man. He is useless, and probably going to compound everybody's problems with that damn dope of his."

I grip the wheel hard and stare straight ahead. "No."

It starts to rain a little. It starts to rain sheets.

"You've come this far. You have come a long way now. You know what it means, to do what needs doing. Ask yourself again, right now and all the time forever, "When what needs to be done needs to be done, *can I do it?*"

I look at Jarrod's battered and weathered and childlike mess of a face in the rearview, the watery wide eyes looking now out the windows at the endlessly passing same tree. At school he could be your show-and-tell if your topic was *useless*, and I bet at least one classmate tried it when he was at school, and I further bet he went along with it just to be accommodating.

"When what needs to be done needs to be done, I can do it, Da."

"That's my boy."

"But I will decide what needs to be done. And Jarrod stays with us."

My grandfather's eyes go mental with more horror than when he saw his dead wife in my sister. Then the wide eyes narrow, a bit, and a bit, until it resembles more disappointment and distaste. Like he's looking at a half-built structure already falling apart from shoddy workmanship.

"That boy," he says, pointing flagrantly at the passenger in back, "is going to be your downfall."

"Am I?" Jarrod says with majestically poor timing. I give him a quick quadro-shush.

I do not reply to Da, just continue on the long, winding, watery road to our destination.

TWELVE

Who are you when nobody is watching? Da asked me.
Is there ever nobody watching? I asked.
Good answer, he said.

THIRTEEN

"I must have fallen asleep," I say.

The car is in a small ditch, with nothing but field visible for miles. It is a monotonous two-lane nothing of a road splitting farms that have corn growing like natural skyscrapers all along the right view, and some hip-high rag balls of common green whatever covering all the land to the left. It is the most boring scape of any land anywhere, and if it does not put you to sleep, then you are some kind of indefatigable driving machine.

Anyway, it's not as if there was any other consciousness in the car to help keep me alert at the time.

"See, I told you this boy was going to be your undoing," Da says as Jarrod climbs down to check the situation because it is after all *his* stolen car.

"What did he have to do with it?"

"Subarus suck" is Da's logic.

"It doesn't look like anything's broken," Jarrod says, lying right down in the muck to look underneath. The pouring rain has stopped and been replaced by moderate rain that feels like many tiny knuckles rapping on my skull.

The right front wheel has lost contact with earth where I tried to jerk the wheel back up in the direction of the road at the last second. The other three are in touch. There is reason to believe two of us may be horsepower enough to get the thing righted while a third one navigates the vessel onto the pavement.

"Da," I say, shaking my head as I say it, "with your hip and all you'll be no good pushing, so you'll need to drive."

"I love to drive," he says, clapping once and crab-walking down the short embankment to the car.

"Yeah." I sigh. "I'm aware."

I make my own way down the slope to the rear of the car, where Jarrod waits, his entire front now lacquered in rich farming mud.

"Feeling strong?" I ask, as the wind picks up and starts blowing sideways into our ears.

"No," he says.

But we all do what we have to do. I explain to Jarrod the concept of rocking a car out of a predicament, rather than plowing it out. I try and coordinate with Da by shouting at him because he is old.

"Da," I say. "On the count of—"

Revvv-revv-revvv.

The man loves to drive.

"Da!" A little louder. "We are going to try rocking—"

Revvv-rev-revv.

"Aw, hell, put it in gear!"

He lets the clutch out, and drops it into first, and Jarrod and I start plowing with all our might.

"Rock, Jarrod, don't plow."

He tries rocking; we rock in opposite rhythm. I adjust, and so does he, so we rock in opposite rhythm. I believe I hear Da making revving noises with his mouth as the wheels throw ever more mud over Jarrod and me. He is enjoying himself so much, I don't think he cares one way or the other whether we get back on the asphalt.

I feel the wheels catch, grab, we fall back.

"This hurts!" Jarrod says.

"Rock, Jarrod."

Jarrod rocks. We push, back off, push, back off.

Revvv-revvv-revv, and *ka-fump*, the car flops up there and rubber hits road.

And keeps going.

Jarrod and I are lying on the lip of the road, where we flopped with the last heave. We watch as Da lights out for the great unknown and his next adventure without a backward glance.

"Isn't he turning around?" Jarrod asks, as we stand up and watch. There is no brake light activity yet.

"It does not appear he is," I say. "And I don't like the way the car's looking, either."

The Subaru is doing a fast-motion little shimmy action all the way down the highway, like a very happy, motorized springer spaniel.

The stretch of road between the farms is long and flat and

straight, so we have a good long look at the end of this par-
ticular endeavor as Da leaves us definitively behind, in the
rain.

Until he hits what is probably a nice wide slick of water-oil
mix, hydroplanes left to right clear across the road, down the
ditch, and into the corn. It looked to go quite smoothly, as
these things go.

"Come on," I say, starting at a full gallop.

"That is a long, long way," Jarrod moans, but follows.

A few seconds later, we see this small figure, out of the corn
fields, up on the embankment, and waving at us to come.

I slow to a stroll.

"Oh, look, he decided he missed us," I say to Jarrod.

"You think he did?" he says. "I bet he did."

I still feel bad for what I did to him before, so in a way
he's lucky now because a certain level of stupidity has to be
punishable.

"Why are you looking at me like that, Danny? Are you
gonna do it again?"

I put an arm around him and knock his head with mine.

It feels like one day and two weather systems have passed by
the time we reach Da. The sun is shining, and he's smoking a
cigarette and waving us in the last hundred yards like we're
in a marathon. A pickup truck has pulled over—after running
right past us—and the driver is smoking and joking with my
grandfather when Jarrod and I finally troop in.

"Sorry, boys," the man says, waving in a way that says feel
free to not shake my hand. "I would have picked you up, but
to be honest, you don't look quite as pick-uppable as the

elder gentleman here. Fact, there is an air of prison-break about your appearance just now."

"It's okay, no problem. But I'll tell you, you could really give us a hand by maybe towing our car up out of the ditch there." It is strictly not in the ditch. It's gone through the ditch and with some force into the field. The corn crop looks like a perfect door has been cut into it.

"Well, um, no. But I tell you what, I could get my gun and go shoot it for you. Because, fellas, she's gone to the great Japanese auto plant in the sky."

"Told them buy American," Da says sadly.

"Ah-*huh*," the man says, nodding, nodding.

He doesn't even look countrified at all, like with the overalls and the chaw and the gun rack? In fact, he looks like one of those lunatic country club golfers with the pom-pom hat and the grape pants. Because that's what he is wearing. And there are golf clubs in the back. Oh, and actually there is a gun rack in the rear window.

"The frame is snapped, right in half."

I turn to Jarrod. "You said it looked fine underneath."

"I'm not a mechanic, Danny."

"It is in two pieces," the man says, supremely amused. "Only thing holding front and back of that machine together is the transmission and the carpeting."

Da has begun walking in the direction we came from.

"Go get him," I tell Jarrod.

Jarrod goes and I speak to the man, up close and personal.

"Listen, I am sorry, but—"

"Whoa there, death breath," he says, and takes two steps back.

And I realize how much further we have drifted from what I thought of as civilization just days ago. I haven't brushed my teeth. As of this moment I don't even think I technically own a toothbrush. We need some money. We need *things*.

We need to get where we are going.

"Can you possibly give us a lift?" I ask.

My comrades have joined us now.

The man crinkles up his nose.

"Smoke?" Da says, offering one to the man.

"Ah," he says to Da as he gleefully takes the cigarette. "We are a dying breed, ain't we? Dying by our own hand, but that's another story. Where are you going to?"

"Lundy Lee," Jarrod says.

"Ooooh," the man says, raising his eyebrows comically. "Queers, artists, or outlaws?"

"Actually," I say, going for as respectable as I can muster, "I'm a philosophy student."

"Ah, all three, then," the man says, making perfect laugh Os of smoke in the air. "I suppose," he says, and we all scramble toward the front cabin, which has two whole benches of room.

"Ah, no no," the man says, looking across the top of the truck at us. "In the bed. And don't touch my golf clubs."

Da heads back to climb in, and the man shouts, "Not you, sir. You're up here with me. Let them filthy young pups roll around back there."

Da has a spring in his limp as he ambles back up front. I can tell he administered himself his afternoon dose while waiting for us to catch up. It reminds me. "One minute," I say to the man as I hop out and run down to the hobbled Subaru. I get to the car, get inside, and clean out our sad little bag of belongings. If I cannot keep my team healthy, wealthy, wise, clean, housed . . .

I can at least keep them on their meds.

"What the *hell* is he saying up there?" I ask Jarrod as I peek up at the conversation going on in the comforts of the cab. The two of them are chain-smoking and laughing and shouting and wildly gesticulating their way through a nonstop Da-fest of tale-telling. That guy seems like the kind of man who holds his own in any exchange of stories, if he doesn't dominate it, but there is no mistaking that this session is all singing, all dancing, Da. I only hope the guy doesn't think turning us into the local law enforcement is in order, and if he doesn't, then maybe he considers the whole thing worth a buck or two donation.

A couple of times I get worried enough to bang on the cab's rear window. When Da looks at me the first time, I give him a turbo octo-shush, which only makes him wave me off and launch right into another killer story to his new pal. The second time, after my knocking frantically, I figure it is futile when the two of them spin in my direction and give me dual, synchronized octo-shushes.

They laugh so hard I fear we are in for the third crash of the day. So I slink back down low, under the big built-in storage chest behind the cab.

The end of August is some of the loveliest weather of the year. If you are not in the open bed of a pickup truck going seventy, northbound when you are already north of probably forty of the continental United States. If you are not already weakened by exhaustion and unwelcome excitement you could only have ever dreamed of before. And especially if you are not a confused and stupid and fragile and helpful and helpless mess of a nowhere man who just happens to be badly in need of his self-prescribed medicine on top of all of the above.

I lie down on the floor of the truck, in front of Jarrod. I back up into him so that as much of my body surface is contacting as much of his body surface as is decently possible. And then a little more. We huddle there that way, for dear life, for survival, for the duration of the trip.

FOURTEEN

Everybody has a kill switch, Da said.

Same as a car with an immobilizer. The power is there, it's just interrupted. You just have to find the kill switch that reconnects that power.

Once you flip your kill switch, you can do anything. Everything you thought you couldn't do, and many things you never even thought of.

What if I don't want to kill anything, I said.

You don't know that until you've flipped the switch.

FIFTEEN

When the big truck finally stops, and the engine cuts, it still feels, underneath me, like the motor is vibrating. I suspect the left side of my body will feel like that for some time now, and my right side will feel like defrosting chicken. Jarrod clings to my back like a baby marmoset as we hear the doors of the comfortable part of the vehicle bang shut, one-two.

Next thing, the two men are hanging over the side of the truck bed, observing us as if selecting tonight's slab of halibut.

I look up at the Golfer, and he looks the way you look when you get off the best carnival rides. Grinning, delirious, stunned, disheveled, possibly a bit nauseous but unwilling to admit it, and ready to sign up for more.

"That is a great American," he says, and I'm pretty sure he's not talking about Buzz Aldrin.

"You are right about that," I say, creaking myself into an

upright position. Without my insulation, Jarrod instantly goes into teeth-chattering mode, sits up, and clings again to my back. Every sinew of the boy quakes like an electric charge is being bolted through him.

"Here," the Golfer says, peeling off business cards for each of us, "I know a couple people in this town. Don't know what you're looking for here—don't know if I want to know, either—but if you mention my name at the ferry office or at the pawn shop called Bread and Waters, these folks will treat you right."

"Thank you," Da says, and the two men hug like two old war veterans parting ways.

"Yeah," I say, hopping over the side. "Thanks for this, and for the lift. You really bailed us out."

"Just being a good neighbor," he says. "Pass it on, pay it forward, whatever."

I help Jarrod down as the Golfer ambles back to his cab, climbs in, and then takes off with a three-toot salute of his horn and a big wave over the gun rack.

We have been deposited in the savage beating heart of the place that is Lundy Lee. We are in front of the Episcopal church, looking straight ahead down the road to the ferry terminal. Straight down the other road to our left is what appears to be the commercial part of the town. To the right is a lot of nothing, leading to a large, clinical-industrial fright of a squat yellow-brick building that automatically makes you feel like walking in the other direction. We walk that way.

It is getting dark, and most places are closed up. We pass a drugstore, a dry cleaner, a fast food shop that has a long menu in the front window, though the one and only scent wafting out of the open front door is boiling grease. That doesn't hurt its popularity any, though, as there are a dozen teenagers pimpling around out front and several more at the counter inside. We pass a Salvation Army thrift shop, right next door to a Salvation Army mission. Every place other than the fast food joint is closed.

There is a very narrow alley running between the two Salvation Army operations.

"I gotta take a leak," Jarrod says.

"Go on, then," I say as he slithers down the alley.

Da and I take up matching poses, arms folded, leaning on the corners of the two buildings. A couple of pagodas, guarding the sacred piss alley.

"What now, Da, do you think?"

"Don't know," Da says, "but I like it here."

"You do?"

"What's not to like? Look, there's the ocean."

He points, across the street and down a couple of blocks, where indeed you can see the open water leading out from the ferry terminal to the wide, watery world.

"So it is," I say. "What are we going to do with it, though?"

"Well, can't drink it. Too salty."

"True enough. But I was thinking more along the lines of you can't sleep on it. We are pretty well homeless right now. We have to work something out."

"We will. This is the exact kind of place where things work out."

"It is?"

"It is."

We wait a bit more, silently, until I run out of patience.

"Well," I say, "nothing is going to get worked out with numpty peeing down his leg all night."

"Maybe he got lost," Da says generously.

"Yeah, maybe," I say, and start making my way down the pencil-straight lane.

When I get to the end, I am greeted by garbage and excrement smells, a Dumpster, and Jarrod stretched out on his back on the ground.

"Hey," I say, rushing to him and kneeling down beside him. His eyes are open and staring at the sky. Otherwise, lifeless. "Jarrod, are you all right?"

"I am now. Lots of all right. Stars are beautiful tonight. And busy."

I look up at the complete cloud cover.

"Yeah, dazzling. Come on, on your feet, Gonzo."

"I'm not gonzo. I'm right herezo."

I yank him up onto his feet. He wobbles, wavers, and finally gets something like righted. I lead him back out of the alley.

Where the other one has vanished.

"Jeez," I say, smacking the side of my head with the heel of my hand. "Stupid, stupid."

"Don't say that," Jarrod says. "If you are stupid, we don't stand a chance. What's wrong, anyway?"

I turn my anger on him. "Do you notice anything missing from this picture?"

Jarrod actually says, "Hmmm," and looks around pensively.

"Ah, come on," I say, yanking him by the arm.

We make our way farther up the strip, passing a closed

insurance broker, an everything-for-a-dollar shop, and a liquor store, which is open but so barricaded and fortified it seems very closed. Da is not in there, anyway.

Then we find ourselves standing in front of a big, caged front window that reads in burnt orange arcing letters, BREAD & WATERS LOANS.

"Hey, it's the place, isn't it?" Jarrod says, pointing. "Haven't we been here?"

"No, we haven't. It's one of the places the Golfer mentioned."

And it appears to be open. And there appears to be an elder gent at the counter, speaking to the young man in charge.

We go in. "Da?" I say, and he turns around to greet us hazily.

"Yes, Young Man?"

"You can't just flit off like that."

"I don't flit. I just walked."

"Still," I say. "I was worried. We don't even know this town and—"

"I have a friend who told me about this place," he says, picking up the Golfer's business card off the counter where he'd slapped it.

"He's a good man," says the guy across the counter, who can't be much older than me. "He was a good friend of my dad's. So that card makes a good introduction."

"I'm Dan," I say, by way of my own introduction. I shake his hand.

"I'm Charlie Waters Jr." he says. "Proprietor of this treasure trove."

"Cool," I say, looking around at all the fancy dresses, musical instruments, power tools, lawn statues, and all that make up the pawnbroker business. "Open kind of late, no?"

"Very irregular hours here," Charlie says. "In this town, pawnbroker is a kind of on-call job, so sometimes I just stick around late. Sometimes I have appointments, late, early. Sometimes I just sleep in the chair." He gestures to a particularly foul-looking thing squatting low behind him.

"Well, okay," I say, "seeing as introductions are made and that card has introduced us nicely, can I ask if you know of a place three wise men might crash for the night?"

"Hmmm," Charlie Waters says. "You mean someplace you would actually want to stay? In Lundy Lee?"

"We are happy to stay someplace we don't want to stay too."

He laughs. "Well, I have some storage space upstairs where I have had company stay before. I suppose I could offer you some floor space and blankets, for just a few bucks."

"Yes," Jarrod says, standing upright with eyes firmly closed.

"I'm quite tired, Young Man," Da says, sounding more childlike than I have heard him yet. As we speak, I see his body packing up, curling his spine forward, making his hip hinge outward rather than forward.

"Thing is, Charlie," I say, "we don't have even a few bucks right now, to be honest."

For such a young guy, Charlie Waters wears an expression that already nothing much surprises him.

"I do happen to be in the loans business," he says, smiling warmly. "It says so right out there on my window."

I sigh because it just keeps getting incrementally more embarrassing.

"Thing is, Charlie," I say, "we don't actually have anything of value, either."

"You guys are the full winning hand, aren't you?" Charlie Waters Jr. laughs.

"I do," Jarrod says, raising his eyelids to half-mast.

"You do what?" Charlie asks.

"I do have something of value," Jarrod says.

"What?" I ask. "Are you sure, man?"

"Sure what?"

"Sure you have something of value? Sure it's a good idea? Sure you can manage to part with it?"

"Well, not *all* of it," Jarrod says with a laugh. "But I can part with enough, for now, till I get sorted out with something else."

Charlie Waters Jr. holds out his hands, palms up, as in *show me what you got*. He's probably had more reason than most to practice that move.

Jarrod steps up to the counter, close to Charlie, to do just that. Bored, disinterested, confused—all that and more— Da wanders the shop now, touching clothes, trying out tin antique fire engine toys and dolls. I have to keep one eye on him while trying to watch the action at the counter.

"No," Charlie says firmly but not unkindly. "I am not in that business."

I feel myself, physically, emotionally, psychically exhausted, deflating. Jarrod's shoulders too slump with the defeat.

"My Da," I say, "he's not well. We've been traveling a long way. A long, long way. He needs rest. We all need rest, Charlie. If you could just see your way . . ."

Charlie is watching as Da goes over the collection of eye-catching dress-up clothes. I think maybe he shouldn't be overhandling the merchandise.

"Stop that, Da," I say, and he whips around to see us staring at him. He's got a Royal Canadian Mounted Police hat on his head and it is so big it goes all twisted around at the swift head turn. He can only see us with one eye now, but he remains frozen.

Charlie's turn to sigh.

"This is why I am a failure of a businessman," he says. He picks up the Golfer's card, waves it around at us, and says, "You can thank this fine guy." Then he turns to Jarrod. "I am going to be sleeping down here tonight. When you get up tomorrow, come right to me, and I will try and steer you someplace where you might be able to convert your merchandise into useable currency. I think I know a guy. And if not him, I am pretty sure this guy knows a guy . . ."

We sleep on a floor that smells like dirt and sawdust that has been lying there since the thirties. Actually, there is something soothing about the smell. Charlie provided exactly what he promised—floor space and blankets—and although I feel a little stiff when I wake up, I could not complain one bit about the night's sleep. It could have lasted a week, it was so deep.

I go to Da to check on him first thing. He is lying, awake, motionless when I approach him.

"How are you, Old Boy?" I ask.

"Stiff, Young Man. And tired."

"Didn't you sleep well?"

"I slept well. But it's the kind of tired sleep doesn't seem to fix anymore."

I help him to his feet. He walks around the empty space, stretching and bending this way and that, working out the kinks. He walks to the dirty picture window facing onto the street, across the street, over the street to the sea beyond.

"Nice place," he says. "Nice, nice place."

I step up beside him to see this nice, nice place.

"Well, the sun is out," I say. "Which is nice."

I turn back to the bundle of blankets that was Jarrod's bedding, and he is not there. "Let's get on out into that nice, nice place and see where it gets us," I say.

When Da and I get downstairs, Jarrod is dealing with Charlie at the counter. Charlie is handing over some bills, and both guys are smiling, satisfied.

"Hey hey," Charlie says when he sees us.

"Hey hey," Jarrod says. He sounds chipper, and even looks and smells better.

"Where'd you get the clothes?" I ask. He looks like a high school track coach now, but his duds are clean and so is he.

"Thrift shop," he says. "And the mission gave me an egg and an English muffin and let me take a shower. In fact, they *made* me take a shower before they gave me the food."

"Sleep well, men?" Charlie asks.

"Great," I say. "Thanks again."

"Happy to help," he says. He and Jarrod have concluded business, and we head out of the shop. "I'm sure I'll see you again," he adds.

"Don't count on that," Da answers.

Out on the sidewalk, Jarrod turns around, all fatherly, and hands me some cash, and Da as well. Not a lot of cash, but some is a sum right now.

"So business went well," I say.

"Business went well," he says. "I went right over there," he says, pointing across the street and a hundred yards up, where the Compass Inn sits next to the North Star Bar. "I was in the North Star, and it couldn't have gone smoother. Pretty busy, too, for so early in the day. Best part, though, best part? When I showed the guy running the place that business card and asked about work, he called the ferry office right away. Right away."

"That's good," I say. "Jarrod, that sounds really good. But don't get your hopes too high. Most places don't usually hire just like—"

"Well, this ain't most places. I ship out this afternoon. Guy told me lots of new guys apply in the morning and ship out by the afternoon. Wild, huh?"

"Can I shower?" Da says, and steps right out into the street, aiming for the bar. I yank him back just before a beer truck rumbles past.

"Sure, Da," I say. "But the shower is this way."

We walk in the direction of the Salvation Army mission.

"Jarrod, what do you mean, shipping out this afternoon? Shipping out to where?"

"Don't know, don't care, didn't ask. I just want to go. And you guys can come too. The man said they need any live bodies I could round up. Seems like they can't fill these jobs no how for some reason. Lucky, huh?"

"Bugger boy," Da says, not even looking toward us.

"Da, shush."

"What? What does that mean?" says Jarrod, more offended than worried.

"Bugger boy. Boats need bugger boys. Bugger boy."

Jarrod looks to me, a little more desperately now.

I silently wave Da off. "He doesn't know anything about it," I say. "Lucky you. You'll land on your feet. This is great news. New life maybe?"

"Maybe. That would be really good, if a little scary, too. Guy in the bar, though, he told me that pretty much everybody on the boats does most of the same what I do, so it's cool either way."

Well," I say, patting him on the back, "good news on top of good news. I am happy for you, Jarrod, I really am."

We reach the mission and stand outside for a few seconds. "Come with me," he says, "on the boats."

"College," I say.

"Postpone," he says.

"No," I say.

"No," Da says, though not sure to what.

We sit at a small wooden table and sip juice and coffee while Da takes his well-earned shower. Then he comes out to find the promised English muffin, plus the drinks. Just like with Jarrod, I am not even offered solids pre-delousing. Da looks happyish, having undoubtedly taken his dosage. Happyish, though, as the pills just seem to get progressively weaker for him. I don't think we'll be buying generic next time.

Jarrod waits with Da while I take my shower. I am quick, but my, what a shower it is. Glorious. Life-giving.

We are all but glowing, the three of us, with renewed vigor and outlook, as we finish up, thank the mission folk profusely, and move on our way.

"Want to go look for some clothes now, Da?" I ask.

"Nope," he says. He points in the direction of the Compass and the North Star.

"Hold on," I say, determined to do at least a small something about my attire. I run into the thrifty, grab a heavy burgundy sweatshirt that says SUFFOLK UNIVERSITY LAW SCHOOL on it and a long, pea-green all-weather trench coat off the rack, a coat just like in all the foggy old spook movies in London. Very practical. I am pulling on the trench coat as I hit the sidewalk and it fits great, if I tie the belt around twice and don't mind a jacket down to my ankles. As it happens, I don't.

"That's your new wardrobe?" Jarrod jokes.

"It's versatile," I say. "All I will need is this and a selection of underwear."

Jarrod leads the way across the street, the newly minted professional sailor with the appropriate side-to-side swagger in his step.

We go into the North Star, where we meet the benevolent businessman and the helpful employment agent/barman and a few early drinkers who couldn't be more polite if we bought them drinks. Which we don't, and won't.

"I have to go," Jarrod says.

"Where?" I ask.

"Over to the terminal. I have to get my uniform, get fingerprinted . . . all the regular new job stuff."

"I see," I say.

"I'll catch up with you later. But don't forget, I leave on the one o'clock ferry. That'll be it, I'll be gone. So if I don't see you before that, make sure you're there."

"Of course," I say. "Wouldn't miss it."

He goes suddenly watery, wobbly. He grabs my hand.

"You wouldn't, would you?" he says. "Everybody needs

somebody to see them off, right? And you're my best friend. You're both my best friends."

Da looks up at the tin, patterned ceiling, then down at the bare wood floor, clearly impatient with this.

"Wouldn't miss it," I say. "Count on it."

"Okay, guys," Jarrod says, excitedly backing away on his way to get fingerprinted and all that other usual new employee stuff.

"Now we can get a drink," Da says, bellying up to the bar.

I follow him, and the bartender says, "ID, please."

I am not bothered, as I really didn't want one. I am happy to stand there while Da savors his own, however.

"Wild Turkey," he says. "And I hope it's the hundred-and-one proof, not that silly eighty-six stuff."

The bartender laughs. "Well, sir, we have both. One just costs a little more."

"Money is no object," Da says, finally certifying his complete departure from this reality.

He does savor it, though, and the pure enjoyment I witness on his face as he does, and as he heads not once but three times over to the small circular porthole window that looks out onto the waterfront, is more intoxicating than if I had my own drink. Even the 101 proof.

"Let's give the next place a try," he says, nodding repeatedly his agreement with his own idea. "I bet they'll serve you a drink. For goodness' sake, you certainly look old enough. You look older than you did yesterday, even, you ol' crock."

"Sure," I say, surfing his wave of good spirits, "let's go, young crock."

SIXTEEN

"Who the hell in this world plays a concertina anymore?" Da says as we sit at a grubby table in the grubby Compass Inn tavern, next to the grubby North Star Bar. Grubby as the place is, just like the North Star you can still look out the backside windows to watch the workings of the grubby harbor and the comings and goings of the ferry.

Da can barely contain his glee. One by one, salty characters attach themselves to us like barnacles, taking up all the spaces around our table. He's like the new kid in the schoolyard everyone wants to get first friendlies with.

The little old crusty in an ancient mariner outfit comes right up and blasts his concertina music for us, at us. It is more like a battle than a performance, though it is hard to tell who is winning. It's also hard to tell what, if any, tune is involved.

"Was that 'Greensleeves' toward the end there?" Da says,

waving his finger at the man. The man's wide-open, toothless, babylike smile suggests that it was.

"Let me buy you a drink," Da says.

"I thought you'd never ask," the man says.

"I *wish* you'd never asked," I say in Da's ear. "You don't have a lot of money, Da. And we don't know what's going to come."

He stands up and pushes my head away as he goes to the bar. At the bar I see him order, then watch as another grizzled seafaring type says something to him. Da fairly leaps into a short, animated telling of something that makes the hardened old soul gasp, cover his mouth in shock-like, then wave the barman over to get Da another shot.

A minute later, Da is sitting again with us, toasting America, the concertina, and life in general. Then, using America as his segue, he starts with the yarns.

"Did I ever tell you . . . ," he says to all these people he has never met before.

Chairs scrape the floor as folks inch closer. Old vertebrae audibly creak as people twist to lean their good ears into the story.

He tells the one about the blinded scientist in Tel Aviv.

He tells the one about setting the nerd's face on fire with thick specs and sunshine.

He tells one about impersonating a jockey and winning a big race on a drugged horse in Bolivia.

A beer shows up in front of him. A few minutes later, a hefty-looking Reuben sandwich appears.

He does not appear to remember me. He shows no sign of awareness, of either my presence or any of the strain and tribulation of the preceding days. He does not even show any of the tiredness he expressed only just recently.

"He'll be absolutely fine," the frightening man sitting on the other side of me reassures me. I look at him, and he speaks from behind a gray walrus mustache and two cheeks with prominent T-shaped scars carved into them. There is nobody here, in fact, without some facial hair. Da's beard has grown in rather fully. "He's got currency here. In Lundy Lee, everybody lives on stories. One way and another, a man with stories gets by very well here. One way and another."

I look at the man while on my other side Da keeps storying away. Oohs and aahs and small claps are the background music as he reaches peaks of spellbinding.

"That is good to know, thank you," I say to the man. He winks reassurance and I see the same T scar on his eyelid.

There is a brief lull in the show, as a couple of people head for the toilets, a couple more head for the bar, and one of the two women in the place comes up and puts her hand on Da's hand. "Don't you dare start again until I get back," she says, unlit cigarette in one hand and the solution in the other.

"I won't," he says, giddy. Probably the first time he's ever been pleased to be asked to stop talking.

I am hoping my first day at the university is half this successful, is what I'm hoping.

"This is what you want?" I ask after tapping his shoulder, after he has shooed me away for the third time. "Is this the place, Da? Is this the time and the place?"

"Valhalla," he says impatiently, shooing me the fatal fourth time.

"You understand, though? That I am leaving you. I am really just leaving you here. And going my own way. For good and for real."

He nods.

"I knew it before you did," he says.

He reaches out and places his hand on the side of my face. He stares at me for several long seconds, truly, I think, appreciating me. Then he gives that side of my face a good, crisp clap, sending me away, finally, finally-finally.

And so it goes just like that. After all. I go. I am shooed, and I go. I put on my trench, tie up the belt, gather my chunky sweatshirt, and I go.

"Nobody dies of peritonitis in this day and age, right? So . . ." goes the beginning of the story he is spinning as I leave.

Outside, I take it in, the town, the everything, and I still cannot fathom it. I curl around to the port side to walk along the grubby, crumbling dockland. The ferry is coming in, rusty tears running down all along its seams.

"Hello, Young Man," Zeke says, startling the ever-loving out of me.

Once more, I cannot fathom it.

"No," I say. "No, absolutely not. No. He has found peace."

"Maybe peace never wanted to be found. Not by him."

"No. He is here now. Everybody tells stories here, so it's all good and fine by everyone here. He has a beard now, like everyone here."

"We'll give him a good shave."

I remember when Da joked about his whiskers, he said just precisely that, that they were going to give him a good, close shave. He made a little zipper-scar gesture at his temple.

"Absolutely not," I say. "The beard looks good. The beard suits him. The beard stays."

Then Zeke says something. Something that works a kind of

sick magic, something that instantly calls to mind Da's words about flipping a guy's kill switch.

"You'll get it, son. Someday, you'll get it."

There is a moment. There are, I suppose, lots of smaller, preparatory moments in your life. But I think there is the one moment where something of you is changed, profoundly, elementally. It probably does not happen to everyone, but that's just because they swerve this way or that way and just narrowly miss it, because it was probably there, out of sight, out of mind.

I feel different before I even do it. The doing of it is almost secondary.

One of the many great things about a rotting old port town is that there is always a chunky piece of wood lying handy when you need it.

I toss my new heavy Suffolk University sweatshirt on the ground behind me and pick up the chunky piece of wood. He smiles at me, almost, almost a laugh.

I crack him, tremendously, right at that temple spot where the zipper scar would go, swinging right through him, the way good, natural hitters do. He drops to the deck, stands like a bleeding, cowering dog on all fours. I need him to look up at me. None of this honorable death baloney for you, mister. He looks up, petrified, horrified, glorified.

He opens his sad little mouth to plead his soulless, meaningless case.

But he doesn't get his chance.

I put down the chunky piece of wood, balancing it on one end between my knees. Then I conclude communications with a beautiful bouquet of wiggling fingers in front of my pursed lips.

"Octo-shush," I tell Zeke. "It's a funny joke. From the office. You remember. Or do you remember? Are you even supposed to remember? Are you *allowed* to remember?"

He doesn't try to answer me this time. He knows we have our answer.

Then I reclaim my chunky piece of wood and I club him. It's done.

He lies there at my feet in more blood than I thought a human body contained. I grab him, roll him, and shove him over the side, into the water. It actually goes *plunk*.

I straighten up, look around, expecting . . . something. I look and look. Even the ferry pulling in, right there, right there so close, gives away nothing.

I feel myself shaking. It only makes sense, though, doesn't it? Big thing there. Nerves are dancing like spit on a skillet. I can feel myself shaking from my feet on up, like I am making the rotting wooden walkway beneath me crumble to bits with it, and then I will fall through and meet Zeke in the water. I feel it in my stomach and my head and even my vision—my eyes themselves are doing something they have never done before, actually physically trembling, juddering, side to side in the sockets, vibrating at the frequency of hummingbird wings. My brain and the backs of my eyeballs are leaning on each other and combining to make a buzz that's a torture.

I extend my hands wide in front of me to look. I close my eyes then, to the juddering. "Stop," I say, as calmly as I can. I open my eyes and watch my splayed hands again and they are shivering, quaking to make Parkinson's seem like stillness. "Stop it," I say, low, firmer. "Stop it now, Young Man," I say, staring, staring, staring at my hands as the shaking slows, slows, calms, finally finishes.

I stare at my hands for minutes now, waiting. I listen to myself, check myself, wait for myself. Stillness. There is a fair amount of blood on my all-weather spook coat. Into the water it goes.

I did this. It was there to be done and I did it.

It has been some time. I look up and around again at the peculiar port town.

If Lundy Lee noticed anything amiss, or if it cared, it has already forgotten.

There's a story for the grandkids, I think.

"Time, Young Man," I say.

I promised Jarrod I would see him off, and I meant it. This outgoing ferry will be him gone now to whatever happens to a guy like him on a boat like that, and good luck to him.

"Maybe, when you get to college," he says, "you can check out and see, maybe they need a caretaker. Then we can be a team again."

The boy and his relentless unfathomable heart does make me smile.

"They might need a caretaker, but probably not as much as you surely do."

"Then there's that. Either way, I see the team reunited."

The team. Unfathomable.

I do wonder if there is such a thing as juvenile dementia. Maybe that's the team we're on, really.

"Come here," I say, and pull him close to me. I drape my new thick burgundy Suffolk sweatshirt around his shoulders.

I feel they are death-bony shoulders. "Try and keep warm, at least," I say.

He pulls the thing on, wrapping himself into it and grinning like I gave him mink.

"You defy all the laws of human nature," I say.

"Well, then, you defy all the other ones," he says, trapping me in a spindly, unexpected kind of creepy hug that feels like the best thing I can remember feeling.

Until it brings on the trembling in me again and I have to shove him away.

"Just go to work, will ya," I shout, turning away as he goes up into the tub of a vessel.

The boat eventually pulls away, as it does a couple of times a day. It goes straight to the Big Island, which by all accounts is pretty small, and then another boat gig takes Jarrod away, farther, from here, from stuff, from me, from old difficulties and almost certainly to a whole bunch of new ones.

He is waving at me, waving madly from the rail of the boat like one of the doomed idiots launching on the *Titanic*. But in this case, he is the only idiot waving, the other passengers and crew showing no interest in the port they are leaving behind or the people they are leaving to it.

I wave at him a little less nuttily, but nuttily enough.

My waving only makes him wave with ever more gusto, and broadening grin.

An utter, unfathomable nut job.

This is why love is for chumps.

S EVENTEE N

Independence, solitude, silence, are all great things.

But hitchhiking, ultimately, is for chumps. It is little wonder hitchhiking is so identified with mass murder. Ten minutes after you have been picked up by one of these jamokes, you want to kill them. Every one of them.

I make it just under halfway before I break down and call my sister to come and bring me home.

She is great for doing it. But I don't feel chatty.

"Is that it?" Lucy says, finally exasperated with me after about a half hour of the clam show. "Nothing? You got nothing for me after all that?"

"Sorry," I say, staring out at the trees I know individually by now. "Thanks for getting me."

"Well, I don't get you, but that's another story. So, you just . . . left him? Just like that?"

"That's what he wanted."

"Hnnn," she says. "What he wanted, huh? Fine, then. I'm cool with that. Nice work."

"Thanks."

We indulge in some more silence until we reach her limit again.

"Did you hear about Zeke?"

Now I turn away from the trees. I feel my face flush just like when I didn't know an answer in school. But I hope she is not paying that close attention to my details. She looks over.

"Watch the road, jeez," I snap.

She watches the road.

"No," I say. "What about him?"

"Dead. Yeah, just like that. They just found him a few hours ago. A mess, apparently. They say he was hill walking, way up there in the jaggedy foothills up north. Fell, apparently, a long way down a cliff face and into a flooded quarry. Very pretty, they say."

I look back to my trees.

"Huh," I say. "Wow. How's Mom and Dad anyway?"

I find out how they are when I meet them on the front porch. It feels like I have been away a year. I would love to get reacquainted with my cozy room and my lovely bed right now.

That won't be happening.

"What's this?" I ask, pointing at what is too obviously my suitcase on the top step. My mother is giving me a strange and tentative hug as I ask.

My father has never been big on answering stupid questions,

so he lets that one lie there. I extend my hand to shake his but instead he hands me this plastic file box sort of a thing. I look at him and wait.

"You should have everything you need in there. There is money. Bank records, paperwork."

I open the box and there is all kinds of blah-blah-blah a person needs when a person has to be running his own life. Some of it I recognize, some I don't.

"Some of this is Da's," I say.

"D. Cameron. If it is D. Cameron, it is for you. There are notes to that effect, which you can read at your leisure. If you need anything else, you know how to reach us."

"I'm not sure I do, actually," I say. Little joke there. Goes over well.

"Call me, Dan," Lucy says. "Okay?"

"Of course," I say.

We stand there, me, my parents, my sister, my belongings, playing out the grand mal seizure of awkward silences. The weight of it all threatens to pull the porch right underground.

"Dad, college doesn't start for another—"

"Best of luck, son."

Pretty unambiguous there, my dad. I pick up my suitcase. Lucy rushes up and breathlessly squeezes me in the hug that I have been seeking, missing, dying for, and I feel myself well up at just the moment when I need to be made of much tougher stuff than that.

This is why love is for chumps.

I suck up my tears the way a little kid sniffles up snot. That's that.

I walk backward down the front steps of my house.

"Is this because I released the old man, Dad?" I ask, in motion.

He nods. "And because I suspect he has released you. I know what he was, Daniel. I won't live with it again."

I stop dead in my backward tracks.

This does not please them. My parents turn and go into their home. Lucy stands there, quivering, waving, blowing me kisses, and staying planted right where she is until I am gone.

"You look like a man who could use a lift," comes a voice from the car that is crawling alongside me.

"I never liked you," I say to Da's old workmate Largs.

"Fair enough, and mutual, Young Man."

"That is not my name."

"Hop in, Daniel. I will drop you where you are going."

"It's just up ahead," I say, "about twelve hundred miles."

"I was thinking more bus station."

I get in, and he goes quiet for a bit, tooling along the streets toward the bus terminal. When he has given me enough adjustment time, he talks.

"Horrible shame, about old Zeke," he says.

"Horrible," I say crisply.

"But that's old men for you. They fall down and die. Happens all the time, they fall down and they die."

"You're not that much younger."

"Ouch." He laughs, a laugh that sounds like train wheels squealing on a bend of track. "I guess I'd better be careful, then, huh? But that's what retirement villages are for, huh?

So they can be safe and not hurt themselves or anybody else. Right?"

"I suppose."

"That is a nice one you found for your grandfather. Perfect, I think."

I snap my head in his direction and all his chummy nonsense bleeds right out.

"You are good, Daniel. But you are not that good. Don't get all worked up, anyway. I meant what I said. It is a perfect retirement village for him. He's safe there, I think. You did damn well there. He's safe and god knows we don't need any more old men falling down and hurting themselves right now. That doesn't do anybody any good, does it?"

To think, I merely hated him up until now.

"No, it doesn't," I say.

He pulls up in front of the manky, desolate bus station, stops the car, reaches into his blazer pocket.

"Why do I want your card?"

"In case you need anything. Just give me a call. And maybe after you graduate, who knows, maybe I can find something for you. There is always a place for a bright young philosopher with hard-world experience, you know."

I give Largs as cockeyed a look as I can manage. Then I tuck the card in my pocket once me and my belongings are out of his car.

EIGHTEEN

Don't forget me, will you? Da said.

How could I? I said. How could anyone forget you?

Ah, but you will, though. It'll happen, probably quicker than you could know.

Not happening, Old Boy.

Don't be stupid, Young Man. Be anything else but stupid. And it's stupid to think you won't forget. And it will happen to you, as well. Probably sooner than you could imagine. We all get forgotten. Don't forget that.

He was right. By the time I got to school, all this was forgotten.

I made it. To the university, to freshmen week, which I remember almost nothing of, to philosophy.

I made it.

I got a roommate who is also philosophy and who smokes

so much dope my computer giggles for ten minutes every time I open it up. He tells me all about his background on the sugar beet farm and I tell him all about mine, the summer camps and the horses and the high school archery team and my six-foot-two girlfriend, and he says "wow" a lot, and "cool," and all the other stuff, the bumpy, prickly, complicated stuff is just lost in the fabulosity of my storytelling.

"What's that bracelet thingy, dude?" he asks, taking my wrist and reading the inscription in the copper.

"It was a gift from my grandfather."

"Wow. Cool. That's deep, man."

"That was him all right. Wow, cool, and deep."

"Is there a story attached?"

"Nope."

See that?

Right again, Old Boy.

All is forgotten.

Nixon PZ 7. L979739 Kil 2012